UNITED
STATES OF
AMERICA

U0084491

金門大橋(Golden Gate Bridge)

Golden Gate Bridge

PACIFIC OCEAN

在 Golden Gate Park 的日式庭院

Golden Gate Park

Japanese Tea Garden

在戶外跳舞的年輕人

Twin Pe

市區電車(Streetcar)

漁人碼頭(Fisherman's Wharf)

San Francisco Bay

歌劇院(Opera House)

FRANCISCO

Opera House

住宅區(Residential Area)

加州豐富的水果

LEARNER'S
AMERICAN TALKS
1

AMERICAN TALKS

PRINT IN TAIWAN

supervisor   :   Samuel Liu
text design   :   Jessica Y.P. Chen
illustrations :   Isabella Chang, Jennifer Lin, Sherling Sue
cover design   :   Isabella Chang

ACKNOWLEDGEMENTS

We would like to thank all the people whose ongoing support has made this project so enjoyable and rewarding. At the top of the list of those who provided insight, inspiration, and helpful suggestions for revisions are:

David Bell
Mark A. Pengra
Rebecca S.H. Yeh
Michelle Chen
Melody Wang
Clement Wang
Stella Yu
Marge Chen
Irene Liang
Jesmine Hwang
Sabrina Wang
Winifred Jeng
Bessie Hsiang
Pei-ting Lin

序 言

　　編者在受教育的過程中，常覺國內的英語教育，欠缺一套好的會話教材。根據我們最近所做的研究顯示，各級學校的英語老師與關心的讀者也都深深覺得，我們用的進口會話教材，版面密密麻麻，不但引不起學習興趣，所學又不盡與實際生活相關。像一般會話書上所教的早餐，總是教外國人吃的 *cereal*（麥片粥），而完全沒有提及中國人早餐吃的 **稀飯**（香港餐館一般翻成 " *congee* "，美國人叫它 " *rice soup* "）、**豆漿**（ *soy bean milk* ）、**燒餅**（ *baked roll* ）、**油條**（*Chinese fritter* ）該如何適切地表達？

　　我們有感於一套好的教材必須能夠真正引發學生的興趣，內容要切合此時此地（ *here and now* ）及讀者確實的需求，也就是要本土化、具體化。

　　兩年多來，在這種共識之下，我們全體編輯群秉持專業化的精神，實地蒐集、調查日常生活中天天用得到、聽得到的會話，加以歸類、整理，並設計生動有趣的教學活動，彙編成 " *AMERICAN TALKS* " 這套最適合中國人的英語會話教材。

　　這套教材不僅在資料蒐集上力求完美，而且從構思到成書，都投入極大的心力。在編纂期間，特別延聘國內外教學權威，利用這套教材開班授課，由本公司全體編輯當學生，在學習出版門市部親自試用，以求發掘問題，加以修正。因此，這套教材的每一課都經過不斷的實驗改進，每一頁都經過不斷地字斟句酌，輸入中國人的智慧。

　　經由我們的示範教學證實這套教材，祇要徹底弄懂，受過嚴格要求者，英語會話能力定能突飛猛進，**短時間**內達到**高效果**。這套教材在編審的每個階段，都務求審慎，唯仍恐有疏失之處，敬祈各界先進不吝指正。

編者　謹識

AT美語會話教本

課程簡介

AT美語 會話教本	程度	適　用　對　象	備　註
ALL TALKS ①②	初級	1. 具備國中英語程度、初學英會話的讀者。 2. 適合高中、高職、五專的初級英會課程。	已出版
AMERICAN TALKS ①②	中級	1. 具備高中英語程度，以前學過英會的讀者。 2. 適合高中、高職、五專的進階英會課程。 3. 大專程度的初級課程。	已出版
ADVANCED TALKS ①②	高級	1. 想進一步充實流利口語，言之有物的讀者。 2. 大專程度進階用。	已出版

　　全套教材分初、中、高三級；每級二冊，全套共六冊。每冊皆根據教育部頒定的「英語會話課程標準」而設計，每冊十四課。因此可配合各校授課的學年長短，作各種不同的組合利用：

(1) 一學年（兩學期）：採用初級教本 ALL TALKS①②，內容包括基礎生活會話及一般常見的實用口語，讓同學們學會用最簡單的英語來溝通，打好會話的基礎。

(2) 二學年（四學期）：採用中級教本 AMERICAN TALKS①② 及高級教本 ADVANCED TALKS①②。這四冊的內容、人物均可連貫，自成系統。程度由淺入深，舉凡一般簡單的問候、招呼語到基礎商用、談論時事、宗教等會話皆包括在內，涵蓋面廣，可讓同學們循序漸進地培養實力。

(3) 三學年（六學期）：採用全套「AT美語會話教本」六冊，利用一系列設計的整套內容，經由螺旋式教學法，也就是在第一學年教完 ALL TALKS，讓同學們稍具基礎之後，第二、三學年再接著教授 AMERICAN TALKS 及 ADVAN-CED TALKS；一面將前面學過的內容加以整合，一面適度地添加程度與課程，幫助同學們溫故知新，兼顧語言使用的正確性與流暢性。

CONTENTS

Lesson 1 Meeting People

Meet people.
Say hello to your friends.

🎧 (A) LET'S TALK

A : Hello, Tom.

B : Oh, John. Hello. How have you been?

A : Pretty good, I think.

B : You look a bit tired.

A : Oh, it's nothing. I was up late last night.
How's your brother doing at college?

B : Quite well. He caught a cold last week, though.

A : Hmm... It is getting cold these days.
Well, I have to run. Supper's waiting for me.

B : OK. It was nice seeing you again.

A : See you then, Tom.

LESSON 1

Conversation practice.
Use what you know.

🎧 (B) LET'S USE

LESSON 1

(C) LET'S PRACTICE

Here are some typical phrases that you should know.

(1) Meeting Friends

1. Good morning. (*use during all a.m. hours*)

2. Good afternoon. (*use from 12 noon to 6 p.m.*)

3. Good evening.
   (*do not confuse with* **good night** — *an expression meaning* **good-bye**)

4. Hello. (*an exclamation of greeting, to attract attention, and of surprise*)

5. Good day. (*means* **hello** *and* **good-bye**)

6. How are you today ? (*stress on* "*today*")

7. How are you getting on ? (*asking degree of success in life, work, etc.*)

8. How are you getting along ?
   (*asking degree of success in relationships*)

9. How are things going ? (*same as* "*How are you ?*")

10. How are you doing ?
    (*asking about health and happiness; same as* "*How ya doing ?*")

11. How's life ?

12. How's everything ?

13. Hi !

14. What's new ? (*asking for news*)

15. Hello there. (*same as* **hello**)

16. I haven't seen you *for ages*. (*i.e. for a long time*)

17. It's been ages since we last met.

18. Long time no see.

(2) Meeting Strangers

19. How do you do ? (*"How do you do ?" is used when meeting strangers. Use before giving your name and as a response to "How do you do ?"*)

20. I'm glad to meet you.

21. I'm pleased to meet you.

22. I'm happy to make your acquaintance.

23. I'm very glad to have the opportunity of meeting you.

24. It's nice meeting you.

25. I've always wanted to meet you.

26. I've been looking forward to meeting you.

27. I'm very happy to know you.

(3) Introduce Oneself

28. May I introduce myself ?

29. Please let me introduce myself.

30. Allow me to introduce myself.
    (*The above sentences should be followed with "My name is Peter Wang." or "I'm Peter."*)

31. My name is Peter Wang.

32. I'm called David.

(4) Introduce to Others

33. David, may I introduce Mary ?

34. Peter, I'd like you to meet Jennifer. (*I'd = I would*)

35. Mr. Chen, let me introduce Mr. Lin.

36. Mom and dad, I'd like to introduce Mary.

37. Mr. Chen, permit me to introduce Mr. Lin. (*permit = allow*)

38. Mike Young, allow me to introduce Jane White.

39. I'll introduce you to Fred.

40. I want you to meet a friend of mine.

41. This is my good friend, Don.

(5) **What to Say When Introduced**

42. How do you do. (*respond with "How do you do."*)

43. I'm very happy to meet you.
(*respond with "The pleasure is (all) mine."*)

44. It's nice meeting you.
(*respond with " It's my pleasure." or " I've heard (so) much about you." or "Nice meeting you, too."*)

(6) **Saying "Good-bye"**

45. Good-bye.

46. Good night. (*use in the evening or at night to express good-bye*)

47. Bye bye.

48. G'bye. (*contraction of good-bye: informal*)

49. Bye. (*less formal than bye bye*)

50. Bye now. (*contraction of "Good-bye for now."*)

51. See you. (*contraction of "See you later."*)

52. See you soon.

53. See you later.

54. So long. (*= good-bye*)

55. See you tonight, then. (*then = in that case*)

56. See you tomorrow.

57. See you again soon.

58. Good-bye till tomorrow.
59. Good-bye for the present. (*rarely used*)
60. I'll see you.

(7) Leaving

61. I think I must go now.
62. I've come to say good-bye.
63. I'd like to say good-bye.

64. Well, it's getting rather late.
65. Well, it's time to get back to work, I suppose.
66. If you'll excuse me, I should be off now.
67. It's time for me to be shoving off. (*informal*)

68. It was real nice meeting you.
69. I truly had a wonderful time tonight.
    (*respond with " I'm glad you enjoyed it. "*)

70. I think I'd better be going. (*I'd = I had*)
71. I've got to be going, I'm afraid.
72. I must run along now.
73. It's time we were off.
74. It's time for me to be on my way.
75. I think it's about time to leave.
76. Then, I think I'd better be on my way.

77. I was delighted to see you again.
    (*you may say " It was a pleasure having you. " for all sentences in* (7))

(8) Leaving Words

78. I shall be looking forward to seeing you again. (*formal*)

79. You must also come over to my place. (*said by the guest*)
80. When shall we get together again ?
81. I hope you'll be able to come again. (*said by the host*)
82. Why don't you drop by and have a chat with us ?
    (*respond with " OK, I will. "*)
83. Remember to look me up if ever you're in Taipei.
84. Don't forget to keep in touch. (*respond with "Of course."*)

85. Say good-bye to the rest of the family for me, will you?
    (*respond with " OK, I will."*)
86. Remember me to your parents / folks.
    (*respond with "Thank you, I will."*)
87. Say hello to your brother.
88. Give my best regards to your father.
    (*respond with "Thank you, I certainly will."*)
89. Give my love to Jim. (*respond with " I'll be sure to."*)

90. Have a good time.
91. Have a good holiday.
92. Enjoy yourself.
93. Take good care of yourself.
    (*the four sentences above are said to the person leaving on a trip*)

94. Good-bye, and good luck.
95. Good-bye, and have a good trip.
96. Good-bye, and have a good time.
97. Good-bye, and all the very best.
98. Good-bye, and thanks for everything.
    (*respond with " You're welcome."*)

* The degree of **formality** in the phrases for meeting, introducing, and leaving is equal to their **length**.

LESSON 1

Exercise

Here are some short dialogues. For each multiple-choice question select the single incorrect answer.

1. A: How are you today?
   B: _____
   (A) Just great, thanks.   (B) I've been here.
   (C) Pretty good, thank you.   (D) Well, not too bad.

2. A: Hello, my name is Tom.
   B: _____
   (A) I've always wanted to meet you.
   (B) I'm happy to make your acquaintance.
   (C) I'm looking forward to seeing you again.
   (D) Hi. How's it going?

3. A: You look a bit tired today.
   B: _____
   (A) Just fine.
   (B) Well, I stayed up late last night.
   (C) That may be. I feel tired.
   (D) Oh, I feel all right, I guess.

4. A: How's your mother doing?
   B: _____
   (A) Yes, she is just wonderful, thank you.
   (B) I'm doing all right these days.
   (C) Yes, she's fine, thank you.
   (D) Well, she's been ill.

5. A: If you will excuse me, I should be leaving now.
   B: _____
   (A) When shall we see each other again?
   (B) It was a pleasure having you.
   (C) Good-bye, and have a nice trip.
   (D) I want you to meet a friend of mine.

6. A： Mr. Lin, permit me to introduce my good friend, Miss Hsu.
   B： _____
   (A) How do you do?
   (B) It's time for me to be on my way.
   (C) I am very glad to have the opportunity to meet you.
   (D) Hello. I've heard so much about you.

7. A： I'll see you tomorrow, then.
   B： _____
   (A) I'll see you then.
   (B) Good night.
   (C) Have a safe drive home tonight.
   (D) When shall we get together again?

8. A： How are you getting on?
   B： _____
   (A) I should get going now.
   (B) I've been feeling good recently.
   (C) I couldn't be better.
   (D) Well, not so good.

9. A： Please give my best (regards) to your parents.
   B： _____
   (A) I'll be sure to do that.
   (B) I don't want to give them your best one.
   (C) Thank you, I will.
   (D) I'll be sure to give them your kind words.

10. A： Allow me to introduce myself. I'm Tom.
    B： _____
    (A) Oh, how do you do, Tom.
    (B) Happy to meet you.
    (C) It's so nice meeting you.
    (D) I'm having a wonderful time.

Lesson 2

Talking about the Weather

Talk to your friends about the weather.

🔊 (A) LET'S TALK

A: What a beautiful morning it is !

B: Yes, but the weatherman said that it won't last.

A: Really? Is it supposed to rain?

B: He said that there was a 40% chance of rain this afternoon.

A: Sounds like it's going to be cloudy.

B: He said it would be windy, too.

A: Well, it looks like I'd better take my umbrella with me to work.

B: Yes. It's so sad to see Summer change into Autumn.

LESSON 2

Conversation practice.
Use what you know.

🎧 (B) LET'S USE

(1)

Sunny   Cloudy   Rainy   Muggy

Snowy   Windy   Tornado   Hurricane
(Typhoon)

(2) **Questions about the weather with how and answers with it.**

How's the weather in spring?
It's rainy, but it can be
warm too.

How's the weather in summer?
It's muggy and it often rains.
Sometimes there is a typhoon.

How's the weather in fall?
The skies are clear and
nights are cool.

How's the weather in winter?
It's cold and often rainy and
windy.

LESSON 2

🎧 (C) LET'S PRACTICE

Here are some typical expressions you should know.

(1) Asking about the Weather

1. How is the weather today?
2. What's the temperature today?
3. How's the climate in your country?

(2) Fair Weather

4. The weather is nice today.
5. It will clear up tomorrow.
6. It's warm.
7. It's fine. (*fine = sunny*)
8. What a lovely day!
9. It's very warm for this time of year.

(3) Heat

10. The days are getting warmer.
11. It's muggy today. (*muggy = warm, damp and close*)
12. It's very sticky today. (*sticky = muggy*)
13. It's terribly hot.
14. It's a scorcher today. (*scorcher = a very hot day*)

(4) Clouds

15. It's been cloudy all morning.
16. It will be foggy tomorrow morning.
17. The forecast is calling for high clouds.
18. Those look like rain clouds.
19. The sky looks ominous. (*ominous = worrying or frightening*)
20. Those clouds look like thunder-heads.
    (*thunder-heads = big rounded clouds that appear before a thunder storm*)

(5) Rain

21. It rained all day today.
22. I love spring showers.
23. Looks like rain. (*i.e. It looks like it's going to rain.*)
24. We will have drizzle tomorrow. (*drizzle = a fine misty rain*)
25. The rain is coming down in buckets.
26. It's raining cats and dogs. (*i.e. a heavy rain*)
27. The typhoon brought heavy rains.

(6) Wind

28. There's a cool breeze this evening.
29. There's a strong wind now.
30. It's gusty right now. (*gusty = windy and blustery*)
31. There will be high winds tomorrow.
32. The wind is blowing at 20 knots. (*knot = unit of speed*)
33. A hurricane hit the southern coast.
34. The wind is picking up. (*pick up = increase in speed*)

(7) Snow

35. It's snowing.
36. We received 10 cm of snow.
37. The snow is deep.
38. I love powder snow.
39. When do you usually have your first snowfall?

(8) The Forecast

40. What's the forecast?
41. The weatherman says it will rain.
42. The forecast is calling for cloudy skies.

LESSON 2

🎧 (D) LET'S READ

Here is a typical ICRT weather report. Read it and answer the questions.

Weather Forecast

The weather forecast for around the island is calling for mostly fair skies with a chance of rain in the mountain areas. This pattern will continue on through the weekend. But by next Monday, be looking for a cold front that will drop our temperatures down to around 12° Celsius. For today and tomorrow look for clear skies with only a slight chance of rain. Temperatures for the island will drop down to 20° tonight in the south, and to 18° up here in the north. Today's high should reach 28° down south and 27° for the north. The current temperature in Kaohsiung is 26°; Taichung 25°; and up here in Taipei, it's 26° centigrade or 80° Fahrenheit.

---

1. What is the forecast for the next few days?
2. What will happen around Monday?
3. Will it become cold or warm on Monday?
4. How cold will it get in Southern Taiwan tonight?
5. What is the current temperature in Taipei?

LESSON 2

Exercise

Look at the map and answer questions about tomorrow's weather in Taiwan.

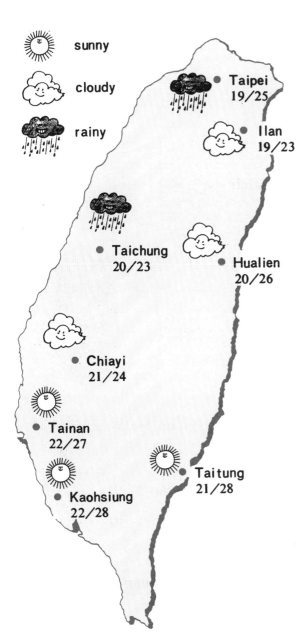

1. Will it be sunny in Taipei tomorrow?

2. What will it be like in Kaohsiung tomorrow?

3. What is the low temperature for Hualien?

4. Will it be cloudy in Taichung tomorrow?

5. What is the high temperature for Tainan tomorrow?

6. What will the weather be like in Taitung tomorrow?

7. Will it rain in Kaohsiung tomorrow?

8. Will Chiayi be sunny tomorrow?

9. Will Ilan and Taipei have the same weather tomorrow?

10. What is the forecast for the southern part of the island?

Lesson  3   Asking Directions

Find your way.
Get directions from strangers.

🎧 (A) LET'S TALK

A : Excuse me, I'm lost. How do I get to Kungkuan?

B : Are you on foot?

A : Yes, I am. I want to know which bus to take.

B : By bus, you will have to transfer.

A : What do I do first?

B : First take bus number 204. It will take you to the International House of Taipei. It's on Hsin Yi Road.

A : Do I transfer buses there?

B : Yes, but you will have to catch the bus on Hsin Sheng South Road.

A : What is the number of the bus to Kungkuan?

B : It's Zero South.

A : That sounds simple.

B : Well, in case you get lost, I'll write Kungkuan in Chinese. Just show this to someone if you get lost.

A : Thank you very much.

B : Don't mention it.

LESSON 3

Conversation practice.
Use what you know.

(B) LET'S LOOK

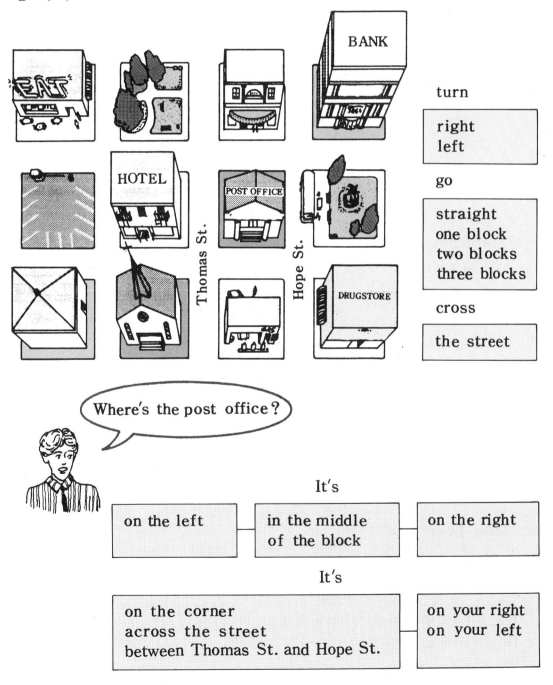

turn

| right |
| left |

go

| straight |
| one block |
| two blocks |
| three blocks |

cross

| the street |

Where's the post office?

It's

| on the left | in the middle of the block | on the right |

It's

| on the corner
across the street
between Thomas St. and Hope St. | on your right
on your left |

LESSON 3

🎧 (C) LET'S PRACTICE

Here are some typical phrases that you should know.

(1) Politely Asking Directions

1. Pardon me. Where is the Grand Hotel ?
   (*pardon me = excuse me*)
2. Can you tell me where the library is?
3. Can you tell me the way to Tun Hua South Road?
4. Sorry to trouble you, but where is the nearest Post Office?
5. Can you direct me to the train station?
6. Can you point me in the right direction?
7. Which way is the train station?
8. I'm trying to find the Post Office.
9. Is there a short-cut ? (*short-cut = a shorter way*)

(2) Getting Confirmation

10. Can I get to the Bank of America from here?
11. Am I heading in the right direction for the YMCA ?
12. Is this the quickest way to the train station?
13. Will this bus take me to National Taiwan University ?
14. Will this road take me there ?

(3) Being Lost

15. I'm *completely* lost. (*completely = entirely, totally*)
16. I've lost my *bearings.* (*bearings = sense of direction*)
17. I have no idea where I am.
18. Where are we ?
19. I've never been here before.

(4) **East , West , South, North**

20. The Philippines are south of Taiwan.

21. Taipei is in the north.

22. Tainan is a southern city.

23. Hualien is to the east of Taichung.

(5) **Giving Directions**

24. Turn right at the next street.

25. Go straight for three blocks.

26. Go two blocks and hang a left.
    (***hang a left / right*** = *turn left / right*.)

27. My house is straight ahead.

(6) **Giving Locations**

28. It's on the next block.

29. Turn left and you will come to it.

30. Go until you reach a tall blue building.

31. The hotel is ***on the left hand side***.

32. It's right behind you.

33. It's on the corner to your right.

34. The bank is next to the post office.

35. The hotel is in front of the bank.

36. The office building is in back of the bank.

37. The restaurant is beside the school.

38. It is up the street from here.

LESSON 3

🎧 (D) LET'S LEARN

Here are some common directions.

1. Go straight down the road.

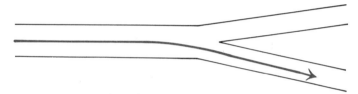

2. You will come to a fork in the road. Bear right.

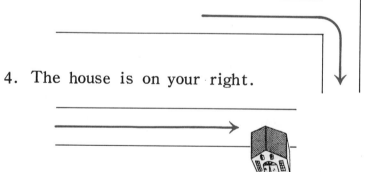

3. Turn right at the end of the road.

4. The house is on your right.

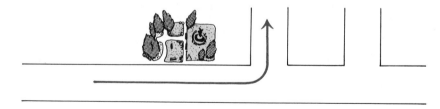

5. Turn left just past the park.

6. Take the first right and the second left.

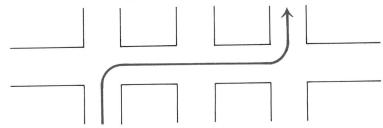

7. Turn left at the second light.

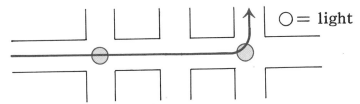

○ = light

8. Cross (over) the bridge.

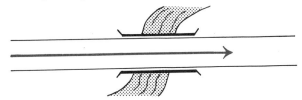

9. Turn right at the first light, and turn left at the first intersection.

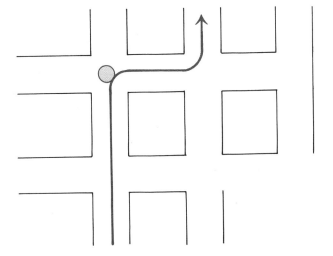

LESSON 3

Exercise

Give directions to the following places.

A. Post Office

B. Bank

C. Park

D. Department Store

E. Movie Theater   ◯ = traffic light

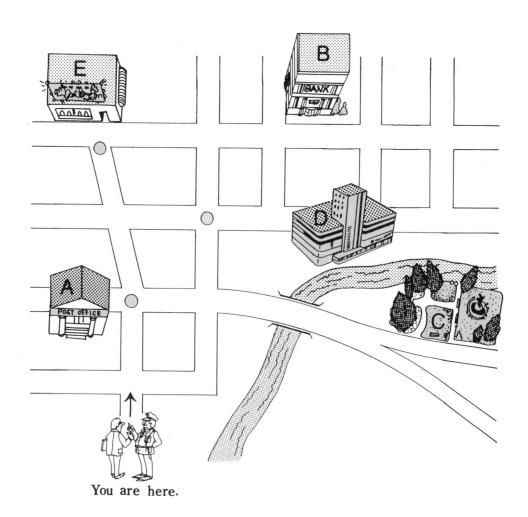

You are here.

Lesson 4   At the Western Restaurant

Speak like a native. Order a western meal.

(A) LET'S TALK

A : This is the restaurant that I was telling you about.

B : It looks nice.

A : Let's sit at that table by the window.

B : What are you going to have?

A : I was thinking of getting a steak or a pizza. I can't decide.

B : Pizza sounds good. Why don't we get a large one and share it?

A : OK. How about a pepperoni pizza?

B : Fine. And I think I'll get a large coke.

A : Hmmmm. I don't care for coke. I'm going to get a beer.

LESSON 4

Conversation practice.
Use what you know.

🎧 (B) LET'S USE

LESSON 4

(C) LET'S PRACTICE

Here are some typical phrases you should know.

(1) **Breakfast**

1. What would you like for breakfast?
2. You're just in time for breakfast.
   (*i.e. it is being served now*)
3. What do you usually have for breakfast?
4. How do you want your eggs cooked?
5. Will you have coffee or tea?
   (*i.e. would you like coffee or tea?*)
6. What kind of omelette do you want?

7. I would like my eggs cooked sunny-side up.
   (*fried but not turned over.*)
8. Can I have my eggs over-easy?
   (*also over-medium and over-hard*)
9. I want my egg poached.
10. Could you bring me some jam for my toast?
11. I want a croissant with butter and jelly.
    (*croissant = French crescent roll*)
12. I want to order a sweet roll and a cup of coffee.
    (*sweet roll = a sweet breakfast roll*)
13. This toast is burnt.
14. Won't you have some more coffee?
    (*i.e. please have some more coffee.*)
15. Would you care for some orange juice? (*polite*)

(2) **Lunch and Dinner**

16. What's for lunch today? (*i.e. what are we having for lunch?*)

17. What will you have for lunch today? (*asked by the waiter*)

18. Dinner time, everybody!

19. How soon'll dinner be ready?
    (*i.e. How long until dinner is ready? soon'll = soon will*)

20. I think lunch is ready. (*i.e. is served*)

21. Set the table for dinner.
    (*i.e. put the utensils and dishes on the table*)

22. I hope you like plain home cooking. (*i.e. typical food*)

23. Please try some home-made bread.

24. This dish is one of my special recipes.

25. Spinach and carrots are good for you. (*i.e. healthy foods*)

26. How do you find the lobster?
    (**How do you find** = What do you think of)

27. Have some more vegetables.

28. I want my steak rare.
    (**rare** = cooked so lightly that the inside is still red)

29. My steak has to be well-done, or I won't eat it.
    (**well-done** = thoroughly cooked)

30. I would like a medium steak.
    (**medium** = between rare and well-done. Also "medium-rare" and "medium-well-done")

31. This steak is under-cooked. Please cook it some more.

32. May I have some steak sauce for my steak?

33. Can I have another piece of roast beef?
    (*less polite than "may I"*)

34. I would like to order a green salad with French dressing.

35. I'll take a tossed salad with blue cheese dressing with my steak. (*tossed salad* = *green salad*)
36. For lunch I like a chef's salad with Russian dressing.
37. May I have a garden salad with Thousand Island dressing?
38. Would you bring me a lettuce and tomato salad with no dressing?
39. I want ambrosia salad to go.
40. I'd like a dish of fruit salad.
41. Your potato salad looks good. I'll have that.
42. Is it possible to get a side order of coleslaw?

43. Can you bring me some more butter?
44. Please pass the salt.
45. Can you pour me another glass of wine?
46. Would you pass the carrots?
47. Would you mind if I had another dinner roll?

48. This casserole is delicious.
49. Your chicken is out of this world. (*i.e. extremely good*)
50. The home-made bread is just scrumptious.
    (*scrumptious* = *extremely delicious or good tasting*)
51. I've never had such a delicious lobster before.

(3) Beverages

52. I take my coffee black. (*black* = *without cream or sugar*)
53. I like my coffee without cream.
54. I'll have tea with lemon.
55. I take two lumps in my tea. (*lump* = *sugar cube*)
56. I'd like a coke with ice.

57. The beer has gone to my head. (*i.e. I'm a little drunk*)
58. I'm feeling tipsy. (***tipsy*** *= a little drunk*)
59. This wine is a cut above average. (*i.e. better than most*)
60. This is a dry wine. (***dry*** *= not sweet*)
61. I like a sweet wine.

62. Would you care for something to drink?
63. What will you have to drink?
64. What's your pleasure? (*i.e. what would you like?*)

(4) Dessert

65. I would like apple pie a la mode. (*i.e. with ice cream*)
66. I want ice cream for dessert.
67. For dessert we'll have chocolate cheesecake.
68. Can you nuke my apple pie? (***nuke*** *= heat with a microwave*)
69. I would like a dollop of whip cream on my pie.
    (***dollop*** *= a lump or blob*)
70. Could you put a dash of chocolate on my pudding?
    (***dash*** *= a small amount*)
71. I have a sweet tooth. (*i.e. I like to eat sweet things*)

(5) The Check

72. Can I have the check?
73. Is the service charge included in the check?
74. Do I pay you or the cashier?
75. Where can I pay for this?

LESSON 4

(D) LET'S EAT

Here is a typical western restaurant menu.

the PLAZA restaurant

MENU

BREAKFAST

Eggs	$ 1.99
fried	
scrambled	
poached	
Cereal with fruit	1.10
hot	
cold	
Waffles	1.59
French toast	1.59
Pancakes	1.59
Toast with butter	.39

LUNCH

Hamburger	2.99
Hot dog	1.49
Sandwich	3.29
roast beef	
ham	
tuna salad	
Pizza	5.99

DINNER

Sirloin steak	8.99
Chicken Breast	5.99
Ham with pineapple	5.99
Casserole	$ 3.99
Pork chops	4.79
Salmon steak	10.99

（All selections come with soup, salad, and bread）

SIDE ORDERS

Tossed salad	1.39
Carrots	.59
Peas	.59
Cheese and crackers	2.39
Potatoes	.79
baked	
mashed	

BEVERAGES

Carbonated drinks	.50
Coffee or tea	.50
Fruit juice	.79
Beer	.99
Wine	1.10

DESSERTS

Ice cream	.79
Apple pie	.79
Cheesecake	.79

● Study the menu. Then form groups of three students. One student is the waiter or the waitress. The other two are the customers.

WAITER : Good _____ . What would you like for breakfast
/ lunch / dinner ?

CUSTOMER 1 : I'd like _____ .

WAITER : Is that all ?

CUSTOMER 1 : No, _____ too. (Yes, _____ .)

WAITER : And what would you like, sir / ma'am / miss ?

CUSTOMER 2 : _____ .

● Listen to the role play and write down what the customer orders.

GUEST CHECK

TABLE NO.	NO. PERSONS	CHECK NO.	SERVER NO.
		755982	
Side order			
Main course			
Dessert			
Drink			

LESSON 4

Exercise

Here are some short dialogues. For each multiple choice question select the single incorrect answer.

1. A : What would you like for breakfast?
   B : _____
   (A) Just toast and coffee.
   (B) I want mine without cream.
   (C) I'll take your brunch special.
   (D) Can I see a menu first?

2. A : What kind of dressing would you like on your salad?
   B : _____
   (A) Ketchup, please.   (B) Oil and vinegar sounds nice.
   (C) Blue cheese, if you have it.
   (D) I would like some thousand island dressing.

3. A : Will you be having dessert?
   B : _____
   (A) No thanks, just coffee is fine.
   (B) Yes, what kind of pie do you serve?
   (C) Spinach and carrots sound delicious.
   (D) I would love a dish of ice cream.

4. A : Are you ready to order?
   B : _____
   (A) Could you give me a few more minutes?
   (B) I don't like that very much.
   (C) I would like a hamburger.
   (D) You haven't given me a menu yet.

5. A : Is there a vacant table?
   B : _____
   (A) Yes, right this way.
   (B) Not for another ten minutes.
   (C) We're completely booked tonight.
   (D) Show me to it, please.

Lesson **5** At the Chinese Restaurant

Speak in the city.
Order your meals in China.

(A) LET'S TALK

A : Hi, John. Care to join me for breakfast ?

B : I'd be glad to. What are you having ?

A : I'm having some hot sweet soybean milk and a Chinese fritter.

B : That looks delicious. But I think I'll have some rice soup instead of the soybean milk.

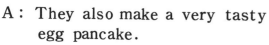

A : They also make a very tasty egg pancake.

B : I think the fritter and the rice soup will be enough. So, how's it going ?

A : I've been quite busy recently with work. How about you ?

B : The same. I have a new client who is never satisfied. But, it's a living.

LESSON 5

🎧 (B) LET'S LOOK

• Ordering in a Chinese Restaurant

1	2	3
Chinese ravioli 〔,ræviˈolɪ〕	steamed dumplings	steamed stuffed bun

4	5	6
Chinese fritter	green onion pie	soybean milk

7	8	9
springroll	Chinese pancake	pastries

* 在美國「春捲」多稱爲 " eggroll "。

10 glutinous rice ball	11 rice soup	12 baked (*wheat*) roll
13 beef noodles	14 beancurd jelly	15 glutinous rice dumpling
16 fire pot	17 won-ton soup	18 eight treasures rice pudding
19 shark fin soup	20 sweet and sour spareribs	21 roast suckling pig

(C) LET'S PRACTICE

Here are some typical phrases that you should know.

(1) **At Home**

1. Watch out！ You've spilled your soybean milk.
   (**Watch out**！ = *Be careful*！)
2. I feel hungry already.
3. Let's eat.
4. It looks good.
5. It smells good.

6. Please help yourself to more.
7. Help yourself to anything you like.
8. Help yourself to some more.

9. I've had enough. (*i.e. I'm full.*)
10. I hope you have had enough to eat. (*said by the host*)
11. I have had more than enough to eat. (*said by the guest*)
12. I'm not a big eater. (**big eater** = *a person who eats a lot*)
13. No, thank you. I'm full.
14. No more, thank you.
15. I think I've had enough.

16. Will you please pass the salt？ (**pass** = *hand me*)
17. Please pass the pepper.
18. May I have some butter, please？
19. Will you clear the table, please？
20. I have a small appetite. (*i.e. I usually don't eat very much.*)
21. No more rice for me. I'm on a diet.

22. I'm starving to death. (*i.e. extremely hungry*)
23. What can I eat that isn't fattening ?

(2) At a Restaurant

24. A menu, to begin with. (*a response to "What would you like ?"*)
25. I'd like to have a bowl of corn soup (*yu-mi t'ang*), a dish of steamed fish, and some spicy chicken (*kung pao chi ting*).
26. We would like four bowls of white rice.

27. There are some restaurants which specialize in Peking food.
28. I really get tired of eating *off the street*.
      (*i.e. at the street stalls*)
29. I get hungry for Szechuan food. (**hungry** = *a craving*)
30. You have to make reservations in advance.
31. I would like to make a reservation for ten tonight at 7.

32. What would you recommend today ?
33. I'd suggest fried oysters.
34. They are selling like hot cakes. (*i.e. sales are very high*)
35. The vegetable chicken sounds wonderful.
36. That's a very good suggestion. I'll try it.
37. How spicy do you want your curry chicken ?

38. Can I take your order, please ? (**take** = *have*)
39. Are you ready to order now ?
40. I don't care for soup. I'd rather have something else.
41. Have you decided on anything ?
42. Just a moment, I'll be right with you.
      (*i.e. I will be at your table in a few moments*)

43. I'll take two orders of Chinese pancakes.
44. Just a bowl of sweet soybean milk, please.
45. How about some Chinese fritters?
    (*how about* = *would you like*)
46. Would you like any soybean milk with your green onion pie?
47. Your pastries look delicious.
48. May I have rice instead of noodles?
49. I'll have tea after my meal.
50. How would you like your soybean milk?
    (*answer with* " *Hot, please.* " *or* "*Cold, please.*")

51. How long will it take?
52. How much longer will it take?
53. I've been waiting for half an hour.
54. I can't wait any longer.

55. Is there a cover charge?
    (*cover charge* = *money taken at the door*)
56. Is the service included?
57. How are the prices there? (*i.e. Are they expensive?*)
58. How is the service? (*i.e. Is it good or bad?*)
59. What are its hours? (*i.e. When are they open?*)

60. This egg isn't cooked enough.
61. This meat is too tough.
62. This meat has gone bad.
63. This has gone bad.
64. This is rotten.

65. Let's split the bill.
66. Let's go halves.

67. Let's go fifty-fifty.
68. Let's go Dutch.
69. Dutch treat, OK?
70. Let me pay my share.
71. Keep the change.

72. The meal was delicious.
73. That was the best meal I've ever had.
74. We'll come again.

75. Bring us a bottle of your best Hsiaoshing wine.
76. Some old Hsiaoshing wine, lemon juice, and some glasses.
77. I would like to take this bottle with me.
78. I asked for a bottle of Taiwan beer.
79. Please bring me another draft beer.
80. Give me a bottle of your best XO.
81. Do you have any Otard V.S.O.P.?
    (*V.S.O.P.* = *very superior old pale*)
82. Would you care for some mao t'ai?

LESSON 5

Here are the most popular Chinese dishes.

(D) LET'S USE

wined chicken	醉 雞
boiled chicken with onion oil	葱油雞
diced chicken with paprika 〔pə'prikə〕	宮保雞丁
barbecued 〔'bɑrbɪˌkjud〕 duck	脆皮烤鴨
stewed pork balls	紅燒獅子頭
sweet and sour spareribs 〔'spɛrˌrɪbz〕	糖醋排骨
roast suckling pig	烤乳豬
shredded pork with chives 〔tʃaɪvz〕	韭黃肉絲
beef with broccoli 〔'brɑkəlɪ〕	芥蘭牛肉
oyster 〔'ɔɪstɚ〕 sauce beef	蠔油牛肉
steamed cod 〔kɑd〕	清蒸鱈魚
stewed fish head with brown sauce in casserole	砂鍋魚頭
braised 〔brezd〕 shark's fin	紅燒魚翅
mixed sea cucumber 〔'kjukʌmbɚ〕	什錦海參
fried shrimp with cashew nuts	腰果蝦仁
cabbage with dried shrimp	開洋白菜
eggplant with garlic 〔'gɑrlɪk〕 sauce	魚香茄子
beancurds with brown sauce	紅燒豆腐
assorted 〔ə'sɔrtɪd〕 cold dish	拼 盤
vegetable chicken	素 雞
Bar-B-Q (*Mongolian Barbecue*)	蒙古烤肉
Taiwanese Cuisine 〔kwɪ'zin〕	台 菜
Szechuan 〔'sɛ'tʃwɑn〕 Cuisine	川 菜
Cantonese 〔ˌkæntən'iz〕 Cuisine	粤 菜
Peking 〔'pi'kɪŋ〕 Cuisine	北平菜

LESSON 5

Exercise

Read each short dialogue. For each question choose the most inappropriate answer.

1. A: How spicy would you like your curry beef?
   B: _____, please.
   (A) I would like it extra spicy
   (B) Mild
   (C) I want mine cold
   (D) Not too spicy

2. A: What kind of soup would you like?
   B: How about_____ soup?
   (A) more   (B) corn
   (C) seafood   (D) hot and sour

3. A: Would you like more tea, sir?
   B: _____, thank you.
   (A) No   (B) Yes, I would
   (C) I want another pot   (D) Would you like one

4. A: Would you prefer spinach or cabbage?
   B: I would like_____.
   (A) cabbage   (B) some more
   (C) spinach   (D) a little of both

5. A: _____would you like this prepared?
   B: I would like it steamed.
   (A) What kind   (B) How
   (C) In what way   (D) Tell me, how

6. A: Please help yourself to anything you like.
   B: Thank you, _____.
   (A) I will
   (B) You are very generous
   (C) that's nice of you to offer
   (D) I'll see what I can do

7. A: _____ do you want ?
    B: I want oolong tea.
    (A) What kind of tea   (B) What
    (C) How   (D) What type of tea

8. A: Another piece of stinky beancurd ?
    B: _____, thank you,_____.
    (A) Yes ⋯ I would like one
    (B) No ⋯ I've had enough
    (C) No ⋯ it can't be done
    (D) Yes ⋯ I'd like another piece

9. A: How do you find the soup ?
    B: _____.
    (A) I found it over there
    (B) I think it's very delicious
    (C) I think it could use more salt
    (D) It's too spicy for me

10. A: What are we having for dinner ?
    B: _____.
    (A) We are having beef noodles
    (B) We can't have it
    (C) We are going to have fish
    (D) I thought we would have pork and rice

Lesson  6 On the Telephone

For pleasure or business.

🎧 (A) LET'S TALK

A : This is China Airlines, Miss Chang speaking.

B : Hello, please connect me to Extension 110.

A : Who is calling, please?

B : This is Mark Jones.

B : Is that you, Mr. Wang?

C : No, sir, Wang is out just now.

B : When do you expect him back?

C : I'm sorry, I don't know. Would you like to leave a message for him?

B : Please ask him to call me back.

C : Yes, sir. Does he have your telephone number?

B : Yes, he does.

C : All right. I'll tell him.

LESSON 6

(B) LET'S DISCOVER

Bob is on the telephone.	Howard Young is answering.	Ted is in the dining room.
Loran is in the kitchen.	Joyce is in the yard.	

- **Answer the questions with *yes*, *no* or *I don't know*.**

1. Is Mike at home?
2. Is Elinor at home?
3. Is Ted in the living room?
4. Is Mike at the library?
5. Is Ted studying?
6. Is Bob on the telephone?

LESSON 6

🎧 (C) LET'S PRACTICE

Here are some typical phrases that you should know.

(1) Hanging up

1. I have to hang up now. (*i.e. I have to go.*)
2. He hung up the phone.
3. I've got to go.
4. Bye-bye.

(2) Time on the Phone

5. She has been on the phone practically all evening.
6. Tell her to get off of the phone because I'm expecting a very important business call.
7. She spends hours on the phone.

(3) Making a Connection

8. My call went through. (*i.e. I made a connection.*)
9. I've been trying to call you up all day long.
10. At last I'm able to get in touch with you.
11. We have a clear line.
12. Her phone is ringing.

(4) Losing a Connection

13. The line's gone dead.
14. We were cut off. I'll have to dial the number again.
15. I was talking to a friend, but the operator cut us off.

(5) Frequent Calls

16. My phone rang like crazy. (*i.e. very frequently*)
17. The telephone was ringing off the hook.

(6) Business Calls

18. Please put me through to the manager.
19. May I ring you back at a better time?
20. What number are you calling?
21. Please give me extension 101.
22. Can I have room 101 please?
23. I forgot to call up Mr. Smith.
24. I promised to call her back at noon.

(7) Promises for Future Calls

25. I'll phone you tomorrow.
26. I'll ring you up this evening.
27. I'll give you a ring this evening.
28. I'll give you a buzz this evening.

(8) Public Telephone

29. Take the receiver off of the hook, and then put in the coin.
30. Put a coin in the slot and then dial the number.
31. I'm at a phone booth.
32. I'm calling from a public telephone.

(9) Bad Connections

33. Please speak more slowly.
34. Please speak louder.
35. I'm sorry, I can't hear you.

(10) **Asking for Future Telephone Calls**

36. Can I get in touch with you by phone?
37. Please contact me by phone.
38. Could you please tell me your phone number?
39. Do you know his phone number?

(11) **Inquiries**

40. Is this Mr. Lin's home? (*formal*)
41. Is this Miss Chen's residence? (*formal*)
42. May I speak to Tom? (*formal*)
43. I'd like to speak to Bill.
44. I'd like to talk to Mr. Jones.
45. May I have a word with Julie?
46. Might I have a word with Julie? (*more formal*)
47. Is Judy there please?
48. Could I talk to Linda, please?
49. Who's calling, please?
50. May I have your name?

(12) **Responses**

51. This is Tom speaking.
52. This is he. (*in response to " Are you Mark "*)
53. This is she. (*in response to " Is Debby there? "*)
54. Mark speaking.
55. This is John here.
56. My name is Julie.

⒀ **Relaying a Phone Call**

57. Tom wants you on the phone.
58. Tom, telephone for you. (*i.e. the call is for you.*)
59. You are wanted on the phone.

⒁ **Saying Someone is Unavailable**

60. He is out. (*i.e. he is not here*)
61. He is not in. (*i.e. he is not here*)
62. He is not at home.
63. He hasn't come back yet.
64. He is away from his desk.
65. I'm sorry, but she's out.
66. I'm afraid she's not here.
67. I think she's gone shopping.
68. Sorry, but she won't be back until Monday.
69. He's on another line.
70. He's on the other phone right now.

⒂ **Wrong Numbers and Long Distance Calls**

71. I'm afraid you have the wrong number.
72. You must have the wrong number.
73. I'm sorry, I think I have the wrong number.
74. Nobody by that name lives here.
75. I'd like to place a person-to-person call to Taipei.
76. I want to make a long distance call.

77. Please hold on.

78. Please hold the line.
79. Will you hold the line?
80. Please hang up. I'll call you back.
81. I'll see if she's in.
82. I'll put you through. (*at the office*)
83. Hang on a minute, please.
84. I'll find out if she's at home.
85. Hold on a minute, please.
86. Hold the line, please.

(17) **A Busy Line**

87. The line's busy.
88. I'll call back later.
89. I'll hold on.

(18) **Taking Messages**

90. Would you care to leave a message?
91. Could you take a message?
92. Would you tell her I rang?
93. Would you ask her to call me back?
94. Can you tell her to ring me when she gets back?
    (*answer with* " *I'd be glad to.* " " *Yes, of course.* " *or* " *All right.* ")

🎧 (D) LET'S READ

Read the passage and answer the questions that follow.

Communication

Unlike Taiwan, America leaves the telephone to private enterprise. Approximately 2,800 independent operative companies exist all over the United States. About four-fifths of the nation's telephones are operated by the Bell System. It comprises American Telephone and Telegraph Company and some 20 operating companies.

Since telephones are nongovernmental in America, it is very easy to get them. You order the telephone and have it installed on the same day. The installation fee and the deposit are reasonable. You can naturally get the deposit back if you cancel service. For these reasons Americans use more than half the telephones in the world and **have** the greatest number of telephones per capita.

Many houses in America have more than one line. This way the father may have a line to his office in his house and the rest of the family will have a phone for their daily use. Now father will not miss important business calls because his wife or children are talking on the telephone.

We live in a time when it is nearly impossible to think of life without a telephone. In the future, most everything we do will be done through this form of communication. We are beginning an age of transition, and soon even letters will no longer be necessary.

● **Answer these questions :**

1. Why is it easy to get telephones in America?

2. About how many independent telephone companies exist in the United States?

3. What company owns most of the telephones in the United States?

4. Why do many houses in the U.S. have more than one line?

5. What does "per capita" mean?

LESSON 6

Exercise 1

Answer each question with a short answer (*Yes, he does / No, he isn't / etc.* or *I don't know.*)

It's 11:40 P.M. The telephone rings and Adela answers it.

A : Hello?
B : Hi, Adela. This is Victor.

A : Victor! How are you?
B : Well, I'm OK, but Mary's sick. She has to go to the hospital.

A : Oh, no! What can I do to help?
B : Well, I have to work and I can't stay home with the children. Can you come here next week?

A : Oh, Vic, I can't. My exams are next week and I have to study. Can the children come here?
B : Sure. They can take the bus on Sunday. It gets to Winfield at 3:30, I think. They don't have to change buses.

A : Fine. Now don't worry about the children, Vic.
B : Thanks, Adela.

A : What are sisters for?

---

1. Does Victor call Adela late at night?

2. Does Mary have to go to Winfield?

3. Does Victor need help with the children?

LESSON 6

Exercise 2

Answer the questions using the words in parentheses.

1. May I speak to Nancy, please?
   (*not here*) _____.

2. Would you like me to take a message?
   (*Dan called*) _____.

3. Is Tom there?
   (*wrong number*) _____.

4. Who is calling please?
   (*Tom*) _____.

5. Please give me extension 448.
   (*hold*) _____.

6. Will you ask her to call me back?
   (*your name*) _____.

7. What is your phone number?
   (*123-4567*) _____.

8. Where can I get in touch with you?
   (*my office*) _____.

9. Is Julie in?
   (*out of town*) _____.

10. When will she be back?
    (*not until Monday*) _____.

Lesson 7 Daily Routines

Speak about everyday life.
Talk about your daily routine in English.

🎧 (A) LET'S TALK

A : Thank you for helping me wash and put away the dishes.

B : It's really no trouble at all. Is there anything else you would like for me to do?

A : Well, is the dining table cleared off?

B : Yes, except for a couple of glasses.

A : Would you grab those for me so I can wash them? And check to see if there is any milk.

B : OK. Here are the glasses. It looks like you are about out of milk. Shall I write milk on the grocery list?

A : Please. And would you write " dishwashing detergent " on there also? It looks like I'll have to go to the store tomorrow.

B : Yes, it does. You've got a long list here.

A : Yea, would you mind helping me?

B : No problem. Are we done in here now?

A : All except for the garbage.

B : I'll take it out.

LESSON 7

Here is Teresa's daily schedule.

🎧 (B) LET'S USE

Read the sentences below and fill in the blank spaces.

1. I get up at_____ .

2. Then I eat breakfast and read the newspaper until_____ .

3. I always drive to work. It takes about 20 minutes. I usually leave
   for work at_____ .

4. I work from_____ to _____ .

5. I usually eat lunch in the cafeteria. My lunch break is from _____
   to _____ .

6. I have dinner at about_____ .

7. I usually watch TV or read until_____ .

8. I go to bed at about_____ .

LESSON 7

(C) LET'S PRACTICE

Here are some useful expressions you should know.

(1) **Morning**

1. Wake up. It's 7 o'clock.
2. Please wake me up at 7.
3. Let me sleep five more minutes.
4. I have to get up early tomorrow morning. I'll have a big day in the office. (*big day* = *busy or important day*)
5. You've got to hurry up !
6. You'll be late for work.
7. Are you still in bed ?
8. You'd better get up. (*you'd* = *you had*)

9. Why don't you get dressed ?
10. I'll go back to bed.
11. You're a half hour (half an hour) late for school already.
12. Come on, it's time to get up.
13. Get a move on. (*i.e. hurry up*)
14. I wish I had gone to bed earlier. I'm so sleepy.
15. Please pull back the curtains.
16. It's stuffy in here. Let's open the window.
17. Breakfast's ready. (*breakfast's* = *breakfast is*)
18. Your breakfast is getting cold.
19. I don't feel like any breakfast. (*i.e. I'm not hungry*)

(2) **Off to work or school**

20. It's time to go now.

21. It's cold, so you'd better put on your coat.
22. Now off you go and don't be late for school.
    (*off you go* = *leave*)
23. It's quite late now. You'd better hurry up.
24. You must hurry or you'll be late.
25. Do you think you can get to the office by 9:00?
26. I always drive to work.

(3) Household chores

27. Shall I keep out of your way?
    (*e.g. while you are sweeping the floor*)
28. May I help you?
29. Would you like me to help you?
    —— No thanks, I can manage.
30. Will you wash the dinner dishes?
31. Be careful with this dish.
32. I'll put the garbage out. (*i.e. take the garbage outside*)
33. I was just going to put the milk bottles out.
    (*for the milkman. He will exchange them for full bottles of milk in the early morning.*)
34. How often do you vacuum the rug?
35. Take the garbage out, will you?
36. I have to mow the lawn today. (*mow the lawn* = *cut the grass*)

(4) Bath

37. Oh no, I got into the tub with my wrist watch on.
    (*tub* = *bathtub*)
38. Don't forget to let the water out. (*i.e. drain the bathtub*)
39. The bath is ready. You can get in now. (*ready* = *filled with water*)
40. Is the bath ready?

41. How is the bath?
    —— It's not so warm.
    —— It's just right.
42. I usually take a shower before dinner.

(5) **Dinner**

43. Dinner is ready, everyone!
44. Take the potatoes and pass them on, will you?
45. Pass the gravy, please.
46. Can I have the peas?
47. Taste your food before you put salt on it!
48. Will you have some more meatloaf?
49. Just another slice, thanks.
50. Take as much as you like. There's plenty.
51. This is a delicious meal.
52. Oh, I'm really full.

53. I can't eat any more.
54. Save some room. I think we have pie for dessert.
55. I think I can make room for that.
56. We are ready to eat, everybody!
57. Let's sit down to dinner. It's ready.
58. I'm starved. (*i.e. very hungry*)
59. Please help yourself. There's plenty.
60. It's delicious.
61. Let me help clear the table. (*i.e. take the dishes from the table*)
62. May I have another roll, please?
63. Would you like another roll or some more vegetables?

(6) **TV**

64. May I turn on the television?

65. Sure. Go right ahead.

66. I'm wondering if L.A. Law is on. It's very popular in Taiwan.

67. I haven't seen this before.

68. I like this documentary.

69. That's public television. They usually show educational programs.

70. There are too many commercials.

71. Change the channel.

72. He's too lazy to get up and switch the channel. (*switch* = *change*)

73. The reception isn't too good.

74. They have a satellite-dish antenna.

75. They have three TVs, so the kids won't fight over the programs.

(7) Night

76. It's nice to put on my clean pyjamas(pj's).

77. The bed's cold.

78. I do hate getting into a cold bed.

79. I'll set the alarm for 7.

80. Turn the lights out, please.

81. You're snoring loudly.

82. I can't get to sleep. (*i.e. I can't fall asleep.*)

83. Why don't you try counting sheep?

84. I go right off to sleep. (*i.e. I fall asleep quickly*)

85. Jim, it's your bedtime.

86. Go upstairs and go to bed.

87. Good night. Sleep well.

88. I'll get out of bed at about 7. (*i.e. I'll rise at 7*)

LESSON 7

(D) LET'S LEARN

Yesterday was a terrible day for Teresa.

- Look at the pictures. Finish each sentence. Use the correct forms of these verbs:

    go to bed   spill   get up   burn   eat   hit   get   is

Teresa usually gets up at 6:45, but yesterday she overslept. She _____ at 9:15. She didn't have time for breakfast, so she _____ an apple in the car. On her way to work, she _____ another car. She finally _____ to the office at 10:45. During lunch she _____ soup on her dress. Later, when she fixed dinner, she _____ it. She _____ too tired to read or watch television, so she _____ at 10:00.

LESSON 7

🎧 (E) LET'S LOOK

Look at this picture and then answer the questions.

● **Questions**

1. Where are these people?
2. Where's Howard Young sitting?
3. What's he reading?
4. What's he smoking?
5. What's Loran doing?
6. What's the little girl's name?
7. Where is she?
8. What's she doing?
9. Where's Ted sitting?
10. What's he doing?
11. Where's Joyce?
12. What's she doing?

LESSON 7

Vocabulary

Here are some typical terms you should know.

(1) **Wake up**

1. early riser
2. wake up
3. get out of bed
4. get up

(2) **Dressing**

1. get dressed
2. dress oneself
3. button one's own shirt
4. take off one's clothes
5. put on one's pyjamas
6. polish one's shoes with shoe polish
7. shave with one's electric razor
8. wash one's hands with soap
9. rinse (them) with water
10. dry (them) with a towel
11. brush one's hair with a hairbrush
12. comb one's hair
13. brush one's teeth

(3) **Bath**

1. bathe oneself
2. take a bath
3. take a shower
4. run the water
5. get into the tub
6. bathtub
7. a bar of soap
8. a can of shaving cream
9. a tube of tooth paste
10. mirror
11. hot water faucet
12. cold water faucet
13. drain plug

(4) **Sleep**

1. pull the curtains
2. set the alarm
3. turn the lights on
4. turn the lights off
5. go to bed
6. get to sleep

(5) **Household Chores**

1. take the garbage out
2. vacuum the carpet (rug)
3. mow the lawn
4. paint

(6) **bed**

1. bunk bed
2. cot
3. hammock
4. single bed
5. double bed
6. blanket
7. bed spread
8. pillow
9. sheet
10. comforter

LESSON 7

Exercise 1

Look at the pictures and write down what he's doing now.

LESSON 7

Exercise 2

Answer these questions.

(1) Answer these questions about yourself.

1. What time do you get up?

   _____

2. What time do you leave home?

   _____

3. What time do you start work?

   _____

4. What time do you have lunch?

   _____

5. What time do you go to bed?

   _____

(2) Complete the following dialogues.

6. A : Do you mind if I listen to some records?
   B : (don't mind) _____.

7. A : Why are you late for work?
   B : (oversleep) _____.

8. A : What do you do after you get up?
   B : (eat) _____.

9. A : What kind of programs do you enjoy watching?
   B : (documentary) _____.

10. A : Do you read when you eat breakfast?
    B : (newspaper) _____.

The Drugstore

Drugstores have more than just medicines.
Find out what they have in English.

🎧 (A) LET'S TALK

A : Let's stop at this drug-store. I need to pick up some things.

B : O.K. I can look around while you shop. You know, we don't have many stores like this in Taiwan.

A : Really? What are the drugstores in Taiwan like?

B : They only sell medicines.

A : Well, we get medicine here, too. That man over there is the pharmacist. That's where you can get your prescriptions.

B : Yes, but look at all of the other things: candy, news-papers, books, toys, and cosmetics. You can even eat here at the lunch counter.

A : Hey, that's a good idea. Are you hungry?

B : I sure am. Let's eat!

LESSON 8

Look at this list of items from a drugstore.
When do we use them?

(B) LET'S LOOK

① Over the counter medicines
   Prescriptions

② Hair care products
       Shampoo
       Conditioner
       Mousse

③ Skin care products
       Cream
       Soap

④ Cosmetics

⑤ Perfume

⑥ Cologne

⑦ Men's bathroom products
       Razor
       Shaving cream

⑧ Deodorant

⑨ Toothpaste

⑩ Bathroom appliances
       Hair blower
       Hair culers
       Electric shaver

⑪ Kitchen products
       Pots and pans
       Utensils
       Toaster
       Coffee maker

⑫ Toys

⑬ General household products
      Wastepaper basket
      Book ends
      Light bulb
      Lamp
      Painting

⑭ Book

⑮ Magazine

⑯ Newspaper

⑰ Paper products
      Typing paper
      School supplies
      Pencil
      Pen
      Office supplies

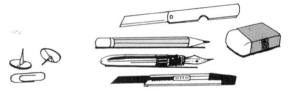

⑱ Cards

⑲ Electronics
      Camera
      Calculator

⑳ Clothes
      T-shirt
      Shorts
      Socks

㉑ Cigarette

LESSON 8

(C) LET'S PRACTICE

Here are some typical phrases that you should know.

(1) **Prescription and Medicines**

1. Please have this prescription made up. (*made up = filled*)
2. Can you make up this prescription for me?
3. Can you give me something for a headache?
4. I'd like to buy some aspirin.
5. I need some aspirin.
6. Do you have any cough drops?
7. Have you got anything for a sore throat?
8. What do you recommend for constipation?
9. Is this good for a headache?
10. How long is this effective? (*i.e. How long does this last?*)

11. How many tablets does this contain?
    (*i.e. How many are there in this bottle?*)
12. How often must I take this?
13. Take one pill with a glass of water three times a day after meals.
14. Take two tablets three times a day before meals.
15. How many pills do I take at a time?

(2) **Sundries**

16. Give me a box of kleenex, please. (*kleenex = facial tissue*)
17. I want a first-aid kit.
18. What can we buy to read in the drugstore?
19. What can we get here for the house?

20. Please give me a pack of razor blades.
21. What kind of razor do you need?
22. I need to get some cigarettes.
23. I need a can of shaving cream.
24. I think I'll get my perfume.
25. I'd like to buy a tube of toothpaste.
26. Can I get mousse here?
27. I don't need a big bottle like that.

28. Do you have any hair curlers?
29. I prefer that toothpaste.
30. Is this bottle of blue ink on sale?
31. Where can I find the cosmetics?
32. What does the lady want to buy?
33. Where are the paper towels?
34. Are they over there at the candy counter?

35. Does this lotion come in a large size?
36. I want to buy some shampoo.
37. Do you want liquid or cream?
38. Oh! I just thought of something else I need. Give me some pencils.
39. Does this store sell lamps?
40. You could get a cheap one at the drugstore over there.
41. Do you have any that are less expensive?
42. Don't you have anything cheaper?

43. This big bottle is a good bargain.
    (**bargain** = *high quality for a low price*)
44. We have this brand on sale. (**brand** = *make*)
45. Is this a good brand?

46. I'll take these.
47. They look good to me.
48. Is this the best you have?
49. Sorry, I don't have anything smaller.
50. I'm sure that's all.

(3) Price

51. How much is that altogether?
52. How much are these?
53. The things I bought added up to $24.50.
54. The roll of film costs $2.70.
55. Here's a twenty. (*a twenty* = *a $20.00*)

(4) At the Lunch Counter

56. What's the soup today?
57. May I have extra mayonaise on my roast beef sandwich?
58. Do you have a lunch special?
59. Hold the gravy on the potatoes. (*hold* = *don't add*)
60. Just a cup of coffee. (*just* = *only*)
61. This is a take-out order.

LESSON 8

🎧 (D) LET'S LEARN

Here are the coins used in America. Circle the amount price of the item.

quarter (＄0.25)　　　　dime (＄0.10)　　　　nickel (＄0.05)
　　　(25¢)　　　　　　　(10¢)　　　　　　　(5¢)

　head　　tail　　　　head　　tail　　　　head　　tail

1. $1.95

2. $2.75

＊ ¢ = cent

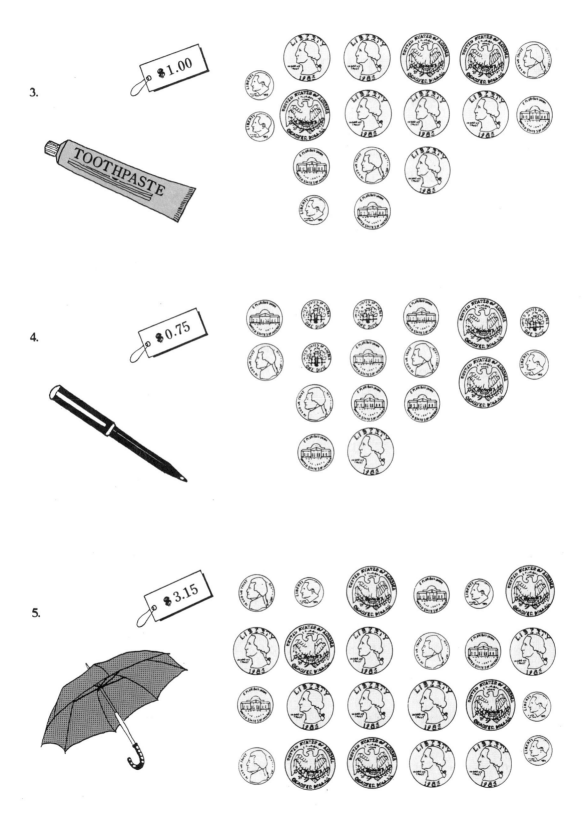

3.

4.

5.

LESSON 8

🎧 (E) LET'S READ

Read the passage, then answer the questions that follow.

The Drugstores in the

U.S.A.

   Americans love convenience. A perfect example of American convenience is the drugstore. You can also see this love of convenience in supermarkets, malls, and "convenience stores" like 7-Eleven. All of these are "one-stop-shopping" places. For Americans, it is much more sensible to get everything you need at one store than at several. This is why you can buy oil for your car at the supermarket. It simply takes less time to get basic necessities, and "time is money."

   Because drugstores are "convenience stores," they sell books, toiletries, kitchen supplies, and just about every household need. They also sell medicines, and many of them have a small restaurant where you can get a little lunch. In some small towns in America, the drugstore is the most popular place for people to meet.

Questions

1. Name some examples of American convenience.
2. What are some of the things that drugstores sell?
3. Why is "one-stop-shopping" sensible?
4. What do many drugstores have?

LESSON 8

Exercise

Put a check mark (√) in front of the sentence with the incorrect counting word for the noun.

1. Shampoo

_____ I would like a loaf of shampoo.

_____ Hand me that bottle of shampoo.

_____ Do you sell tubes of shampoo here?

2. Soap

_____ I can't find the cake of soap.

_____ Would you bring me another bar of soap.

_____ Would you like another hand of soap?

3. Toothpaste

_____ I would also like a tube of toothpaste.

_____ Can I have a head of toothpaste.

_____ Hand me that package of toothpaste.

4. Pots and pans

_____ I bought my wife a set of pots and pans.

_____ I want a piece of pots and pans.

_____ I used to have a box of pots and pans.

5. Cigarettes

_____ Care for another bar of cigarettes?

_____ I want to buy a carton of cigarettes.

_____ I want a package of Marlboro cigarettes.

Lesson

A Trip to the Supermarket

**Buy what you want.
Let's enjoy shopping.**

🎧 (A) LET'S TALK

A : OK, Lisa. We have to buy a lot of food and we have to finish fast. I have to study.

B : Here's the list. Let's divide it.

A : That's a great idea! You get the milk, cheese, beef, chicken and eggs. I can get the potatoes, onions, oranges, apples, tomatoes, bread and coffee.

B : Fine, but where are the eggs?

A : They're over there near the milk.

B : OK.

About five minutes later.

B : Well, I have everything. What about you?

A : I can't find the coffee.

B : Let's ask that man.

A : Excuse me, sir. Where's the coffee?

C : It's over there next to the tea.

A : Oh, where's the tea?

C : It's next to the coffee.

LESSON 9

(B) LET'S USE

Answer the questions according to the picture, then ask and answer questions with a partner.

1. Where's the milk?
   It's next to the eggs.
2. Where are the grapes?
   They're next to the bananas.

3. Where's the ice cream?
   It's near the yogurt.
4. Where are the pears?
   They're near the kiwi.

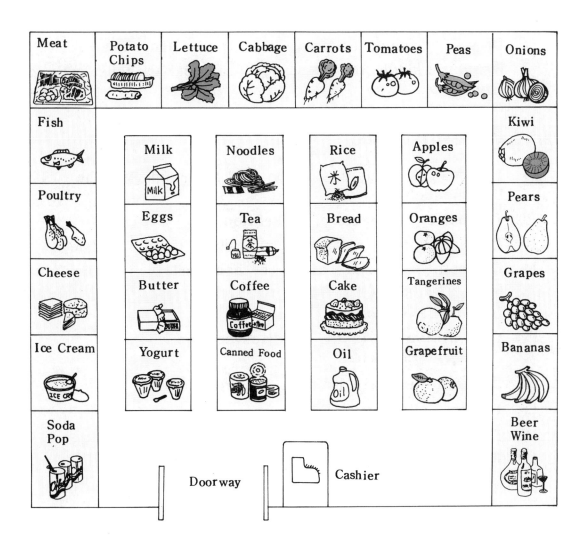

LESSON 9

🎧 (C) LET'S PRACTICE

Here are some useful phrases you should know.

(1) Asking Where a Product Is

1. Where is your laundry detergent?
2. Do you have any cold soda pop?
3. You're out of butter. Is there any more?
4. I can't seem to find the eggs. Can you help me?
5. I'm looking for the eggs. What aisle are they in?
6. Do you sell shoe laces anywhere in the store?
7. Would you kindly tell me where I can find the toilet paper?
   (*polite*)

(2) Locations of Products

8. The soap is in aisle 3 on the left hand side, on the bottom shelf.
9. The butter is in the dairy section.
10. The eggs are in aisle 8, about halfway down the aisle.
11. The potato chips are along the back wall.
    (*i.e. in the back of the store*)
12. It's at the end of aisle 10.
13. You will find it in the sundries section.
    (**sundries** = *miscellaneous items*)
14. If it's not in aisle 10, then we are out of it.
15. The cake mix should be on the top shelf.
16. The ice cream is in the frozen foods case.
17. It's near the meat section.

(3) Phrases of Quantity

18. I want four bottles of oil.
19. I would like two cans of soup.
20. She bought a carton of milk.
21. Please get me a carton of eggs.
22. Would you like to buy a loaf of bread ?
23. I'll take a pound of oranges.

24. The supermarket has only five bottles of wine left.
25. Give me a kilo of bananas.
26. I want two heads of cabbage.
27. Would you buy me three bunches of bananas ?
28. I need to buy a case of beer. (*case* = *24 bottles, cans, cartons*)

(4) Speaking to the Cashier

29. What is the total ? (*total* = *total amount*)
30. How much does this cost ?
31. Will you accept a credit card/personal check ?
32. How much will that be ? (*i.e. What is the total amount* ?)
33. I have some coupons.
34. Would you put this in a bag ?
35. I won't be needing a bag.
36. Can I have a receipt ?
37. Do you have change for a 1000 NT bill ?
38. Do you have a larger bag ?
39. Would you double-bag my groceries ?
    (*double-bag* = *put one bag inside each other for added strength*)

LESSON 9

🎧 (D) LET'S LOOK

Here are count and non-count nouns you should know.

(1) **singular and plural forms of count nouns**

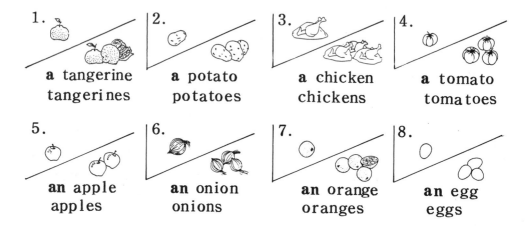

1. **a** tangerine
   tangerines
2. **a** potato
   potatoes
3. **a** chicken
   chickens
4. **a** tomato
   tomatoes

5. **an** apple
   apples
6. **an** onion
   onions
7. **an** orange
   oranges
8. **an** egg
   eggs

(2) **noncount nouns**

9. milk   10. cheese   11. meat   12. bread   13. coffee

(3) **ask and aswer questions**

A : What's this ?
B : It's an egg.

A : What's this ?
B : It's milk.

(A)   (B)   (C)   (D)

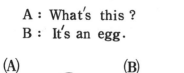

LESSON 9

🎧 (E) LET'S LEARN

Practice quantity words in part one, then tell what each noun is in part two.

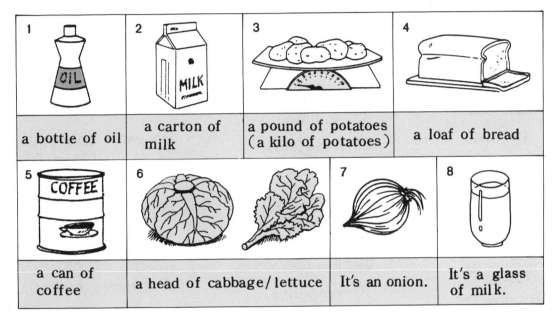

1	2	3	4
a bottle of oil	a carton of milk	a pound of potatoes (a kilo of potatoes)	a loaf of bread

5	6	7	8
a can of coffee	a head of cabbage/lettuce	It's an onion.	It's a glass of milk.

(2)

1 _____

2 _____

3 _____

4 _____

5 _____

6 _____

LESSON 9

Vocabulary

Get more out of shopping by knowing these terms.

(1) <u>Foods</u>

1. apple
2. banana
3. bread
4. butter
5. carrot ['kærət]
6. cheese [tʃiz]
7. chicken
8. coffee
9. egg
10. fish
11. frozen food
12. fruit
13. grapes
14. ice cream
15. meat
16. milk
17. oil
18. onion ['ʌnjən]
19. orange
20. pear [pɛr]
21. pea [pi]
22. potato
23. spaghetti [spə'gɛtɪ]
24. tea
25. tomato
26. vegetable ['vɛdʒətəbl̩]
27. kiwi
28. cabbage ['kæbɪdʒ]
29. lettuce
30. tangerine [,tændʒə'rin]
31. yogurt

(2) <u>The Supermarket</u>

1. dairy section
2. bakery
3. cold case
4. aisle
5. shelf
6. meat section
7. poultry section
8. seafood section
9. beer and wine section
10. fruit and vegetable section
11. paper goods
12. feminine hygiene ['haɪdʒin]
13. household products
14. toilet paper
15. grocery cart
16. canned goods
17. prepared foods
18. baking products
19. check-out stand

(3) <u>Supermarket People</u>

1. cashier
2. baker
3. butcher
4. grocer
5. stock boy

LESSON 9

Exercise 1

First read the dialogue. Then respond to the statements on the following page with *"That's right,"* *"That's wrong,"* **or** *"I don't know."*

Mike is at home. He's talking to his mother.

A : Mike, here's the grocery list.

B : Oh, Mom, I can't go to the supermarket. I have to meet Bob at the park.

A : Sorry, Bob's working and you have to go to the supermarket.

B : Oh, Mom, I can't go to the supermarket. I'm not feeling well.

A : MIKE !

B : OK, Mom. Where's the list?

Mike is at the supermarket and he can't find the grocery list. He's calling his mother.

A : Hello?

B : Hi, Mom.

A : Yes, Mike?

B : I can't find the grocery list.

A : Oh, no! Well, listen and write another list.

B : OK. I'm listening.

A : Potatoes, carrots, coffee, a can of soup, a carton of milk and a pound of pork. Oh, and a loaf of bread, a pound of cheese and a lot of fruit.

B : OK, Mom. See you later.

1. Mike is at the park with Bob.
2. Bob is working.
3. Mike is sick.
4. Mike's mother has to call Mike.
5. Mike has to write another list.
6. Mike has to buy chicken.
7. Mike has to buy milk.
8. Mike is buying apples and pears.

Exercise 2

Match the picture to the word. Write the correct number below each picture.

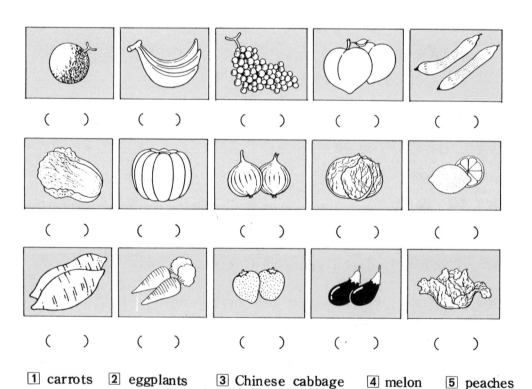

1 carrots   2 eggplants   3 Chinese cabbage   4 melon   5 peaches
6 sweet potatoes   7 onions   8 strawberries   9 cabbage   10 lettuce
11 cucumbers   12 lemon   13 bananas   14 grapes   15 pumpkin

Lesson 10  In the Airport

Go on a trip.
Use English at the airport.

(A) LET'S TALK

A : Your ticket, please. A window or an aisle seat, sir ?

B : A window seat, please. Also, I'd like a seat in the nonsmoking section.

A : Please put your bags on the scale.

B : OK. I hope my bags aren't over-weight.

A : No, you're OK. Here's your boarding pass, sir.

B : What gate do I go to ?

A : You'll be boarding from gate number 12 at 11:30.

B : Thanks a lot.

A : Have a good flight, sir.

LESSON 10

Conversation practice.
Use what you know.

🎧 (B) LET'S USE

- **Now use these phrases in the conversation :**

1. Can I see your customs declaration, please ?
2. May I see your yellow books, please ?
3. Can I see your bags, please ?
4. May I see your disembarkment card, please ?
5. Can I see your baggage claim tag, please?
6. May I see what's in your suitcase, please ?

LESSON 10

🎧 (C) LET'S PRACTICE

Here are some useful expressions you should know.

(1) Choosing a Seat

1. I would prefer a window seat.
   (*a window seat = a seat next to the window*)
2. I'd rather have an aisle seat.
   (*an aisle seat = a seat next to the aisle*)
3. I'd like a window seat.
4. I'd like a seat with a good view.
5. I'd like a seat in the front(middle, rear) of the plane.
6. I would like a seat in the smoking section.

(2) Boarding Gates and Ticket Counters

7. Where's the boarding gate for TWA flight 201?
   (*TWA = Transworld Airlines*)
8. Where's the Pan American ticket counter?
9. Where's gate 13?

(3) Checking Departure Times

10. I'm taking flight 21. Is it departing on time? (*i.e. as scheduled*)
11. Flight 21 has been delayed.
12. TWA 388 has been delayed for 30 minutes.
13. Will the plane take off on time?
14. Is the flight for Seattle leaving on time?

(4) Baggage

15. This is a carry-on.
    (*carry-on = a piece of luggage that is carried on the plane*)

16. I'm carrying this bag with me.
17. What's the charge for excess baggage?
18. How much would it cost to send it unaccompanied?
19. Is there a fine for over-weight baggage?

(5) Questions at Customs

20. How long do you intend to stay? (*intend = plan*)
21. How long will you be staying?
22. Are you here on business or pleasure?
23. Do you have any animals or vegetable matter? (*matter=things*)
24. Do you have anything to declare?
25. What countries have you been to in the last three months?
26. Are these cigarettes for your own use?
27. Do you have any tobacco or alcohol?

28. May I see your passport, please?
29. Passport, please.
30. Can I see your customs declaration form?
31. I'm sorry but your visa is not valid. (*i.e. no good*)
32. May I see your vaccination certificate?
33. Do you have a yellow book? (*yellow book =vaccination certificate*)
34. Open your bags, please.

(6) Responses at Customs

35. I'll only be here a few days.
36. I'm here for sightseeing.
37. I have nothing to declare.
38. I'm here on business.
39. I have only my personal belongings.
40. These cigarettes are for my personal use.
41. I'm a tourist.

LESSON 10

🎧 (D) LET'S DISCOVER

The airport terminal.
Read the passage, study the drawing, and answer the questions.

Many people have never been through an airport. If you are one of these people, here is what you have to do before you get on the plane, and after you get off.

First, you need to have an airline ticket. You can buy it from your travel agent or from the ticket counter at the airport (A). Next, you must pay the airport tax at the airport tax counter (B). Now it is time to go to the check-in counters (C). At the check-in counter your baggage will be checked in and you will be given a seat number and boarding pass. After checking in, you can go through customs and immigration (D), and then on to your gate (E) to board your plane.

After getting off your plane, you move from your gate (E) to the baggage claim area (F). After getting your bags, you go on to customs and immigration (G). Finally, you are in the arrivals waiting area. Here there is a currency exchange bank (H) and plenty of tourist information.

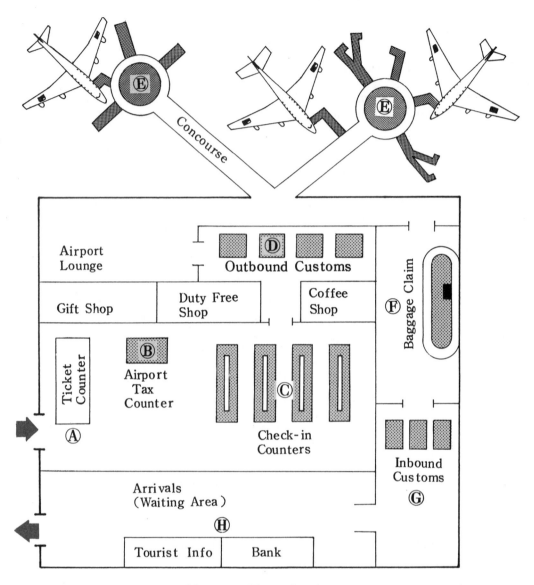

Airport Terminal

1. What three things must you do before going through customs?

2. Can you buy a ticket at the airport?

3. When do you go to the baggage claim area?

4. What kinds of things can you find in the arrivals waiting area?

5. Where do you get your seat number?

LESSON 10

Vocabulary

Here are useful terms for the airport.

(1) The Airport

1. airport terminal
2. check-in counter
3. ticket counter
4. customs
5. immigration
6. quarantine 〔'kwɔrən,tin〕
7. duty free shop
8. airport lounge
9. baggage claim
10. tourist information counter
11. transit room
12. boarding gate

(2) Customs

1. passport
2. visa
3. embarkation card 〔,ɛmbɑr'keʃən〕
4. disembarkation card
5. customs declaration form/slip 〔,dɛklə'reʃən〕
6. vaccination certificate 〔.væksə'neʃən〕

7. immunization card 〔,ɪmjənə'zeʃən〕
8. yellow book
9. personal effects
10. body check

(3) Baggage

1. hand baggage
2. unaccompanied baggage
3. excess baggage charge
4. claim tag

(4) Ticket

1. seat number
2. plane ticket
3. excess baggage ticket
4. boarding pass
5. flight coupon 〔'kupɑn〕

(5) Plane

1. flight number
2. domestic 〔də'mɛstɪk〕 flight
3. international flight
4. first class
5. economy class

LESSON 10

Exercise

Read the conversation and select the correct word for each space.

A : Well, I'm leaving for Hong Kong tomorrow.

B : Oh, that's right. What time do you have to be at the airport ?

A : Well, my plane takes _____ (up, off, to) at 8:00 a.m. so I plan to get there around 7:00.

B : You'll have to get _____ (up, off, to) early. Have you got an alarm clock ?

A : Yes, I do.

B : Say, can you look _____ (out, down, up) John when you get there ?

A : I have his phone number. I could call him _____ (off, out, up) from the airport.

B : That's a good idea. Maybe he'll drive out to pick you _____ (out, up, in).

An Airplane Flight

Get your English off the ground.
Use it on the airplane.

🎧 (A) LET'S TALK

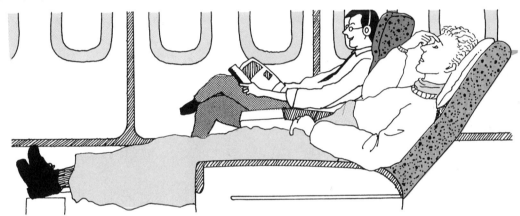

A : Yes, sir ?

B : I feel sick. Could you give me something, please ?

A : Just a moment, sir.

*　　　　*　　　　*

A : Here you are. Take two of these. You should feel better in a few minutes.

B : I hope so.

A : If the pills don't help, don't hesitate to call me.

B : Thank you for your trouble.

A : Maybe you should take a nap.

B : That's a good idea.

A : I'll bring you a blanket and a pillow. These will make you comfortable.

B : Thank you very much.

LESSON 11

Here are some typical phrases you will hear and say on an airplane.

🎧 (B) LET'S USE

LESSON 11

🎧 (C) LET'S PRACTICE

Here are some typical expressions you should know.

(1) **Talking to the Stewardess**

1. Will you show me to my seat, please?
2. Would you help me with this seatbelt, please?
3. May I have a pillow, please?
4. May I change my seat, please?
5. Will we be landing on schedule? (*on schedule* = *on time*)
6. When do we land in Chicago?
7. How long does it take to fly across the United States?

8. Where are we flying above now? (*i.e. Where are we?*)
9. Is a meal served on board? (*on board* = *on the plane*)
10. I'd like a glass of water, please.
11. Could I have tea instead of coffee, please?
12. I don't feel very well.
13. I'm all right now.
14. I'm sorry to cause so much trouble.
15. Please excuse me.

(2) **Listening to the Stewardess**

16. Welcome aboard Pan Am flight 720.
17. This plane is scheduled to take off at 9.
    (*scheduled* = *is supposed to*)
18. Take-off has been delayed.

19. Flight No. 20 is expecting to reach New York half an hour behind schedule.

20. Are you comfortable?

21. How do you feel when the airplane drops into an air pocket? (*air pocket* = *a down current of air*)

22. How do you like your trip by air?

23. Ladies and gentlemen, we are about to land at Charles de Gaulle Airport. Please fasten your seat belt.

(3) Talking to Other Passengers

24. When do you think we will be landing?

25. What is the in-flight movie? (*in-flight* = *during the flight*)

26. Do you think this bag will fit under the seat in front of me?

27. Would you mind if I sat next to the window for a while?

28. Can I borrow a pen to fill out my disembarkment card?

29. How much do the headphones cost?
(*note*: *You usually pay for headphones on flights*)

30. Have you flown on this airline before?

31. Are you flying all the way to New York?

32. Is this your first time in an airplane?

33. Where is the life-preserver?

LESSON 11

🎧 (D) LET'S LOOK

Look at the words below and point to them in the picture.

1. baggage compartment	11. steward	21. reclining button
2. seat	12. pocket	22. safety belt
3. curtain	13. life preserver	23. cockpit
4. screen	14. stewardess	24. business-class seats
5. signboard	15. airsick	25. first-class seats
6. table-release button	16. airsickness bag	26. window
7. table light	17. pillow	27. economy-class seats
8. call button	18. table	28. cuisine 〔kwɪ'zin〕
9. air hole	19. blanket	29. toilet
10. captain	20. ash tray	

LESSON 11

🎧 (E) LET'S LEARN

Time with after, to and past.

a. It's five past six.

b. It's quarter to one.

c. It's quarter past eleven.

d. It's half past two

e. It's twenty-five to four.

● **Say what time it is.**

1.

2.

3.

4.

5.

6.

LESSON 11

Exercise 1

Read the dialogue and answer the questions that follow.

We are on Flight 987 from New York to Los Angeles. I am sitting next to an old woman. She looks worried and nervous.

"Good afternoon," I say. "My name's Helen Miller. Are you going to Los Angeles?"

"Yes," she says. "This is my first flight."

" I go to Los Angeles every month on business," I say. " It's a nice city. Are you excited?"

"No," she says. " I'm nervous. Very nervous."

" I understand," I say. "Who's meeting you in Los Angeles?"

" My son," she says.

I look at the woman. She doesn't look very happy. "Are you hungry?" I ask.

"Yes," she answers. "Do they serve lunch on this plane?"

" Of course," I answer, " They serve a good lunch, but first they serve something to drink. Would you like a glass of water?"

" You can have water," she says, "but I need a strong drink."

Questions :

1. Where did the flight originate?
2. Where is the plane going?
3. Does the woman have a daughter in Los Angeles?
4. Is the woman very excited?

LESSON 12

Exercise 2

Complete the following dialogues using the words in parentheses.

1. S : Would you like to purchase any duty-free items?
   P : (carton of cigarettes) _____ .

2. P : Do you have any news magazines on board?
   S : (Time and Newsweek) _____ .

3. P : When are we going to take off?
   S : (just a few minutes) _____ .

4. P : How long does it take to fly to America?
   S : (about 13 hours) _____ .

5. P : When do we land in Seattle?
   S : (9:45 a.m.) _____ .

6. P : Where can I put this bag?
   S : (under the seat in front of you) _____ .

7. P : I'm going to throw up.
   S : (airsickness bag) _____ .

8. P : Is this flight on schedule?
   S : (right on time) _____ .

9. P : What is the in-flight movie?
   S : ("Rain Man") _____ .

10. P : Is lunch going to be served soon?
    S : (shortly) _____ .

Lesson 12 Invitations

Making an invitation.
Get together with a friend.

(A) LET'S TALK

A : I'd like to have you come to my house tomorrow evening if you are free.

B : Well, I have nothing in particular to do. What time may I come?

A : Is six o'clock convenient for you?

B : Yes, but isn't it dinner time?

A : Yes, it sure is. I'm inviting you to dinner.

B : That's very nice of you.

A : Mom and Dad also want you to dine with us. They're looking forward to having you tomorrow evening.

B : Well, I'd be delighted.

A : Now, I'll be expecting you around six tomorrow evening.

LESSON 12

Make a dialogue using the pattern sentences and the pictures below.

🎧 (B) LET'S USE

(1) A : I was wondering if you'd like to go to _____.

　　B : I wish I could, but....

| my birthday party next Friday | a cocktail party tomorrow | my graduation ceremony |

(2) A : Would you like to go _____?

　　B : Thank you. I'd love to.

| picnicking with us | camping with my family | fishing with me |

(3) A : I'd like to invite you to _____.

　　B : That sounds like fun.

| a basketball game next week | a movie this weekend | an automobile show tonight |

LESSON 12

🎧 (C) LET'S PRACTICE

Here are typical phrases that you should know.

(1) Making An Invitation

1. I'd like to have you dine with me. (*dine = eat dinner*)

2. Will you be able to have supper with us ?
   (*supper = dinner or small meal before going to bed*)

3. I'd like to invite you to a party.

4. Won't you have a cup of coffee with me ?

5. Will you call on me some time next week ?
   (*call on = make a brief visit*)

6. Will you please come to the tea party at three this afternoon ?

7. Will you be able to come to our dance party this evening ?

8. Would you like to go to the baseball game with me next Sunday afternoon ?

9. We would like to have you go with us on a picnic next weekend.

10. How about having lunch with me ?

11. I was wondering if you'd like to go swimming with us.

12. We're going to have a few friends over on Wednesday, and we'd love for you to come.

(2) Accepting An Invitation

13. Yes, I'd love to.

14. Yes, I'd like to. (*not as strong as " I'd love to. "*)

15. Thank you very much, I'd be glad (happy) to.

16. Yes, with pleasure.

17. Thank you for inviting me. I'm sure I can come.
18. It's very kind of you to invite me.
19. That would be fun.
20. That sounds like fun.
21. I'd be delighted to go with you.
22. Thanks, I'll be happy to be present.
23. It looks like it's going to be a wonderful weekend. Thank you.

(3) Politely Refusing An Invitation

24. Thank you very much, but I don't have the time.
25. Thank you, but I'm afraid I'm tied up on Sunday.
    (*tied up = busy*)
26. I'd like to, but I'm afraid I can't.
27. I'd like to go so much, but I have another engagement.
28. I wish I could, but I have to study hard for the exam.
29. I am awfully sorry, but I have other plans.
30. That's very kind of you, but actually I'm afraid I'm rather booked up on Wednesday.
    (*booked up = no free time*)

31. Oh, what a pity! I'd love to, but you see the people next-door are taking me out for the day.
32. If you don't mind, I'd rather not. I've got a bit of a headache.
33. I'm afraid I won't be able to, because I'm not feeling very well today.
34. I wish I could accept your invitation, but I have to go to Taipei on business.
35. I wish I could, but I'm afraid I won't be able to make it this time. (*make it = come*)

LESSON 12

(D) LET'S PLAY

Here are the rules for the game .

1. Get five pieces of paper and write "yes" on three of them and "no" on the other two.

2. Divide the class into two teams.

3. Have one student from the A-team choose a student from the B-team.

4. Have the A-team student ask the B-team student a question.
(Write the examples below on the blackboard)

5. For an answer, the teacher should select one of the pieces of paper randomly and hold it up.

6. Record the response on the blackboard.

7. Now have a B-team student ask an A-team student a question.

8. Continue until everyone has had a chance to play. The winner is the team with the most yeses.

------ **Example** ------

1. Would you like to go to the movies with me?

2. Will you meet us at the movie theater?

3. Won't you come to the party with me?

4. Will you be able to go with me to the disco?

5. I was wondering if you would like to have coffee with me.

6. Can you go with me to the ball game?

7. Do you have time to go for a walk?

8. May I call on you sometime next week?

9. I'd like to invite you to dinner. Can you come?

10. Please come with me to see a movie.

LESSON 12

Exercise

Read the passages, then use what you learn to complete the dialogues.

┌─────────────── **Invitations** ───────────────┐

When you make an invitation you are asking for someone to meet with you at a certain time and place. Spoken invitations are fine for most occasions. At all times the invitation is made only to the person invited. It is bad manners to make an invitation in front of someone who is not invited.

If you accept the invitation, you should thank the person, express your joy in coming, and then find out the details of the occasion. But if you refuse or cannot accept an invitation, you must first apologize for not coming and then give a reason why you cannot accept it. Finally you should thank the person for the invitation.

Situation 1

A : We're planning on having a housewarming party. Could you come over this Saturday?

B : _____ . What time would you like me to come?

A : _____ .

B : _____ .

Situation 2

A : _____

B : Oh, I'm sorry, but _____ .

Lesson 13 Western Holidays

Speak with your friends.
Celebrate the holidays together.

(A) LET'S TALK

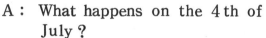

A : The 4th of July falls on a Monday this year.

B : Good. That means we'll have a long weekend.

A : What happens on the 4th of July?

B : All kinds of things. There are parades, fireworks, parties, concerts....
Would you like to go see the parade down Main Street?

A : Yes, that sounds like fun.

B : Good, then we can go together.

A : What time does it start?

B : At 1:00.
After the parade, there is a community picnic.
And in the evening there'll be fireworks.

A : I love fireworks. We also have them in Taiwan on Double Tenth Day, which is our National Day.

B : You'll like these. Everybody in town goes.

LESSON 13

Conversation practice.
Use what you know.

🎧 (B) LET'S USE

LESSON 13

(C) LET'S PRACTICE

Here are some typical holiday phrases you should know.

(1) **Holiday wishes**

1. Happy New Year !
2. A very Happy New Year !
3. Happy Easter !
4. Have a joyous and happy Christmas.
5. Merry Christmas !
6. Merry Christmas and a Happy New Year.

7. Happy Holidays ! (**Holidays** = *Thanksgiving, Christmas, and New Year's*)
8. Season's Greetings. (*said during the Holiday season*)
9. Wish you a wonderful Easter.
10. Happy Thanksgiving.
11. Happy Fourth of July !
12. Happy Halloween !
    (*Most holiday wishes are made by placing happy in front of the holiday's name.*)
13. Trick or treat. (*said by children on Halloween*)

(2) **Replies**

14. Thank you.
15. Thank you, same to you.
16. Thanks. And you, too !
17. Thank you. You, too !
18. Thank you very much. The same to you.
19. Give my best to your family.
    (*The most common response is "Thank you" followed by the holiday wish. e.g. Thank you. Merry Christmas.*)

LESSON 13

🎧 (D) LET'S DISCOVER

Here's how many Americans spend their holidays. Read the text and answer the questions that follow.

New Year's Day (*January 1*)

New Year's Day is always the first day of the year. On New Year's Eve, many people go to parties. At midnight they celebrate the new year with horns, cheers, and kisses. In some cities, people gather to count down the seconds until midnight.

float

Many people make New Year's resolutions. They list their faults or bad habits and resolve, or promise, to change these during the year. A typical resolution would be: I resolve to stop smoking.

New Year's party

Easter
(*On a Sunday between March 22 and April 25*)

This is the Christian holiday that celebrates the death and resurrection of Christ. It is not on the same day every year, but is always on a Sunday.

Easter Bunny

Children dye and decorate eggs and put them in Easter baskets with candy. Other eggs may be hidden for children to hunt and find. Many children believe that the Easter bunny brings the eggs and candy.

Easter eggs

Memorial Day
(May 30 — observed the last Monday in May)

This is the day that Americans remember the men and women who gave their lives for their country. At this time people place flowers on the graves of servicemen. Many areas have parades or other patriotic programs.

Tomb of the Unknown Soldier

Independence Day *(July 4)*

This is the birthday of the United States of America. It is the anniversary of the adoption of the Declaration of Independence by the Continental Congress in 1776.

fireworks display

Independence Day, or the Fourth of July as it is commonly called, is celebrated with contests, picnics, parades, and patriotic programs. The highlight of the day is the fireworks display. Unlike Taiwan, many cities will not allow the sale of fireworks to the public.

witch

Halloween *(October 31)*

This is traditionally said to be the night on which ghosts and witches can be seen. Children often dress up on this night as ghosts or witches and make lanterns out of pumpkins. They then go from door to door saying "trick or treat". To avoid having tricks played on them, people

Jack-O-Lantern

give the children candy, fruit, or money. A trick is something bad, like writing on their door with chalk.

Christmas bells

Thanksgiving
(Fourth Thursday in November)

Thanksgiving is a typical American holiday that marks the beginning of European settlement in America. The first Thanksgiving feast was held in 1621 to offer thanks for plentiful crops, and to celebrate the end of the fall harvest. Today it is the day appointed to give thanks to God.

Thanksgiving feast

Most people celebrate Thanksgiving by eating a big turkey dinner, attending church services, and spending the day with their families.

Christmas *(December 25)*

The most important holiday in the United States is Christmas. For all Christians, Christmas is a time of great joy, for it marks the birth of Christ.

Christmas tree

Americans start preparing weeks ahead for Christmas. They buy gifts for their family and friends and decorate their homes. The most important decoration, of course, is the Christmas tree.

Santa Claus

Christmas day is a day for family reunion. The family comes together and sits down to a large meal in the afternoon. Some eat turkey, some eat ham, others eat roast beef. It is a day to attend church, listen to Christmas Carols, open presents, and relax.

snow flake

Questions

1. Which holiday remembers the men and women who gave their lives for their country?
2. On what holiday can you see ghosts and witches?
3. What is the most important holiday in America?
4. Which holiday has decorated eggs and a rabbit?
5. Who do Americans give thanks to on Thanksgiving?

🎧 (E) LET'S SING

Learn the Christmas Carol "Silent Night" and "O Christmas Tree" in English.

1. SILENT NIGHT

Silent night, Holy night,
All is calm, all is bright,
Round yon Virgin, Mother and Child,
Holy infant, so tender and mild,
Sleep in Heavenly Peace,
Sleep in Heavenly Peace.

2. O CHRISTMAS TREE

O Christmas tree, O Christmas tree,
With faithful leaves unchanging.
Not only green in summer's heat
But also winter's snow and sleet.

O Christmas tree, O Christmas tree,
With faithful leaves unchanging.

LESSON 13

Exercise

Look at the list of U.S. holidays in the left column. Find these holidays in the word puzzle on the right and circle them. The words can go forward, backward, up, or down.

Christmas

Columbus Day

Easter

Halloween

~~Independence Day~~

Labor Day

Memorial Day

Mother's Day

New Year's Eve

Thanksgiving

Valentine's Day

```
N E W Y E A R S E V E V A H S
D E A R Y S L O G A H T R A P
E Y A D S U B M U L O C B L A
P N W E R V L N I E E D Y L E
E S T R X L O V M N O R I O L
N A R O L A B Y D T H L O W E
D M N S Y A D L A I R O M E M
G T I A Y P Y R A N L A B E R
I S S M O M E R X E S T R N E
U I H G N I V I G S K N A H T
I R S Q L A B O R D A Y E A S
N H T U U B H A P A F O D L A
G C H A S O A R I Y E A R O E
S A I T R Y A D S R E H T O M
I N D E P E N D E N C E D A Y
```

Lesson 14 Chinese Holidays

Speak with your friends.
Talk about the holidays of China.

🎧 (A) LET'S TALK

A : What are you going to do for New Year's?

B : My wife and I are going down to Taichung to my parents' house for a family reunion. Then we're going to go to her parents' house the next day.

A : When do you have to be back to work?

B : Not until next Monday.

A : Did your company have a big weiya party?

B : We sure did! After the big dinner, we had a draw for prizes and I won a portable cassette player.

A : Wow! My company gave us a big dinner, too. Well I've got to go now. I'm shopping for some new clothes.

B : I'm going to do the same tonight at the night market. See you later.

A : Bye.

LESSON 14

Conversation Practice.
Use what you know.

(B) LET'S USE

LESSON 14

🗣 (C) LET'S PRACTICE

Here are some phrases you should know.

(1) Asking about vacation plans

1. What are you doing for Lunar New Year?
2. Do you have any plans for Lantern Festival?
3. What will you be doing this holiday?
4. Have you made any plans for the holiday?
5. Will you be going home over the holiday? (*over = during*)
6. Are you going to be eating stuffed rice dumplings?
7. What will your family be doing this New Year?

(2) Talking about holiday plans

8. We're going to go home for Lunar New Year.
9. I plan to go to the temple with my family.
10. She's going to eat moon-cakes and gaze at the moon. (*gaze = look at*)
11. I intend to go to the Dragon Boat Races.
12. My family is going to make lanterns.
13. I intend to get a lot of rest over the holidays.
14. We will be having a family reunion.

(3) Asking about a past holiday

15. What did you do for Lunar New Year?
16. Did you have fun at the Dragon Boat Races?
17. Did you eat a lot of good food over the holidays?

18. What did you do over the holidays?
19. Did you and your family get together during the holidays?
20. Were you in Taichung over the holidays?
21. Did you get a rest over the holidays?

(4) **Talking about the past holiday**

22. My family and I went to the temple together.
23. I went home for a family reunion.
24. We all ate moon-cakes and gazed at the moon.
25. John and I went to the Dragon Boat Races.
26. I relaxed over the holiday.
27. I watched TV and ate a lot of food over New Year.
28. We made lanterns and went to Lungshan Temple.

(5) **Talking about the present holiday**

29. What a lovely New Year.
30. The lanterns look so beautiful.
31. I love eating moon-cakes.
32. It's nice to be home for the holiday.
33. The fireworks are spectacular!
34. I'm glad you could join us for the holiday.
35. I love family reunions.

LESSON 14

🔊 (D) LET'S LOOK

Here is basic vocabulary for the four biggest holidays.

1. Lunar New Year

| "Red Envelope" and "Lucky Money" | Fire-crackers New Year's Greetings | New Year's Couplets Dragon & Lion Dance |

2. Lantern Festival

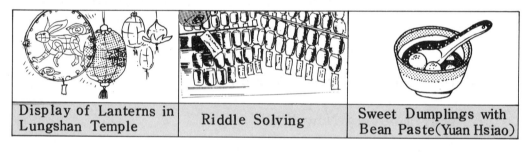

| Display of Lanterns in Lungshan Temple | Riddle Solving | Sweet Dumplings with Bean Paste (Yuan Hsiao) |

3. Dragon Boat Festival

| Stuffed Rice Dumplings | Dragon Boat | Incense bag |

4. Mid-autumn Harvest Festival

| Moon-cakes | Lady in the Moon | Gazing at the Moon |

LESSON 14

(E) LET'S READ

Read the passage, then answer the questions that follow.

Lantern Festival

This festival falls on the 15th day of the first lunar month (first moon). It marks the end of the Lunar New Year. At night people carry around lanterns which have New Year's couplets written on them. They are said to bring good luck in the coming year.

Dragon Boat Festival

On the fifth day of the fifth moon people gather to watch the colorful "Dragon Boat Races," and eat rice dumplings. This day commemorates the death of Chu-Yuan, a poet who drowned himself to protest the policies of his king. In order to keep the fish from feeding on his body the people of the village threw rice dumplings (chung-tze) into the river.

Mid-Autumn Harvest Festival

A festival falls on the 15th day of the 8th lunar month. On this day people get together to gaze at the "Lady in the Moon" and eat moon-cakes. According to legend, Chang-Eh, the wife of an ancient Emperor, drank an "Elixir of Immortality" and flew to the moon. She is still there, and on this night her beauty shines the brightest.

Questions
1. What does Lantern Festival mark?
2. Who drowned himself to protest the policies of his king?
3. What is often eaten for the Harvest Festival?

LESSON 14

Exercise

Here are some short dialogues. For each multiple-choice question select the single correct answer.

1. A : What are you going to do over the holidays ?
   B : _____
   (A) I went to the temple with my family.
   (B) I am going to go to the temple with my family.
   (C) I intended to go to the temple with my family.
   (D) I had gone to the temple with my family.

2. A : What did you do over Lunar New Year ?
   B : _____
   (A) I watched TV and rested.
   (B) I am going to watch TV and rest.
   (C) I am planning on watching TV and resting.
   (D) I hoped to watch TV and rest.

3. A : Did you have plans for the Mid-Autumn Harvest Festival ?
   B : _____
   (A) Yes, I ate some moon cakes.
   (B) Yes, I was eating some moon cakes.
   (C) I had been eating some moon cakes.
   (D) Yes, I was planning on eating some moon cakes.

4. A : When are you going to go home ?
   B : _____
   (A) I had planned on leaving home on Monday.
   (B) I am intending on leaving home on Monday.
   (C) I will go home on Monday.
   (D) I went home on Monday.

5. A : _____
   B : We will be having a family reunion.
   (A) How was your holiday ?
   (B) What will you be doing over the holiday ?
   (C) Did you have a nice holiday ?
   (D) What were you and your family doing over the holiday ?

Editorial Staff

- **企劃・編著** / 陳怡平
- **英文撰稿**

  Mark A. Pengra・David Bell

  Edward C. Yulo・John C. Didier
- **校訂**

  劉　毅・葉淑霞・陳威如・王慶銘・王怡華

  林順隆・林佩汀・陳瑠琍・喻小敏・項福瑩

  梁艾琳・王慧芬・黃正齡・鄭淳文・蕭錦玲
- **校閱**

  Larry J. Marx ・Lois M. Findler

  John H. Voelker・Keith Gaunt
- **封面設計** / 張鳳儀
- **插畫** / 林惠貞
- **版面設計** / 張鳳儀・林惠貞
- **版面構成** / 蘇淑玲
- **打字**

  黃淑貞・倪秀梅・吳秋香・徐湘君

●學習出版公司門市部●

台北地區：台北市許昌街 10 號 2 樓 TEL：(02)2331-4060・2331-9209
台中地區：台中市綠川東街 32 號 8 樓 23 室
　　　　　TEL：(04)2223-2838

American Talks ①

編　　著 / 陳 怡 平
發 行 所 / 學習出版有限公司　　　　　☎ (02) 2704-5525
郵 撥 帳 號 / 0512727-2 學習出版社帳戶
登 記 證 / 局版台業 2179 號
印 刷 所 / 裕強彩色印刷有限公司
台 北 門 市 / 台北市許昌街 10 號 2 F　　☎ (02) 2331-4060・2331-9209
台 中 門 市 / 台中市綠川東街 32 號 8 F 23 室　☎ (04) 2223-2838
台灣總經銷 / 紅螞蟻圖書有限公司　　　☎ (02) 2795-3656
美國總經銷 / Evergreen Book Store　　☎ (818) 2813622
本公司網址　www.learnbook.com.tw
電 子 郵 件　learnbook@learnbook.com.tw

售價：新台幣一百八十元正

2002 年 11 月 1 日一版六刷

ISBN 957-519-120-X